MW01502529

# The Spouse Stealer

Copyright © 2010 by Mark Francis Schwab

© 2010 American Publishing & Distribution Company

Library of Congress Control Number:    2010913829
ISBN:          Hardcover        978-1-4535-7713-4
               Softcover        978-1-4535-7712-7
               Ebook            978-1-4535-7714-1

This is a work of fiction. Names, characters, places and incidents either are the product of the author's imagination or are used fictitiously, and any resemblance to any actual persons, living or dead, events, or locales is entirely coincidental.

This book was printed in the United States of America.

**To order additional copies of this book, contact:**
www.TheSpouseStealer.com
79270

Mark Francis Schwab has written tourism news stories, poetry and fiction since his college days at the State University of New York at Buffalo.

Mr. Schwab served as a journalist on the Oakland Tribune in California, Public Affairs Director for the Zoological Society of Buffalo, Director of Tourism for the Buffalo Area Chamber of Commerce, and appointed by-then Governor Hugh Cary as Chairman of the "I LOVE NEW YORK Summer Festival." Later, Governor Pataki appointed him Deputy Director of ILNY. Also, he was one of the chief tourism architects of "OHIO, The Heart of it all."

Mr. Schwab also owned his advertising and public relations agency much of this time, writing headlines and copy for an international client base such as Waste Management, Frigidaire, WESCO, Rotary Power, Cardinal Health and Bry-Air.

Today he resides in the Adirondack footprint, working on two more books of fiction containing seven historically based short-stories each: The High Peaks and Saratoga Times.

*Author's Note:*

*This is fiction.*

*The book is dedicated to my professors at the State University of New York at Buffalo's English, Art, Science and Education Departments, with whom I've studied, enjoying their interpretations of The Masters. I loved studying with Irving Feldman, the Norton Anthology recognized Poet. Thank you UB.*

*Also, in fond memory of my father, Joseph Francis Schwab Sr., Esq., brother Jeffrey Francis, and still-living brother, Joseph Francis Jr., Esq, LL.M—all UB Graduates who have inspired me on my path for writing poetry and fiction.*

*And lastly, to thank those special friends with my moments of grandeur, love and frustration as I wrote and edited everything.*

# The Spouse Stealer

Mark Francis Schwab

# CONTENTS

# CHAPTER ONE

## *Sailor's Talk*

THE SUMMER SUN was warming a crisp morning air as I sat on the eastern shores of Lake Erie's Canadian shoals, contemplating unbelievable misgivings of knowing an actual spouse stealer and how many lives were infected by such devious and manipulated actions of stealing another's loved one, a spouse. That time in my life was "life's a bitch and then you die."

How could anyone be so contemptuous for planning that? The sheer thought of stealing someone's spouse for their own relationship, no matter what the costs to the other parties involved, can only be realized when it happens to you, personally.

Strangely, she had done it twice before in front of my eyes. These two bought-and-paid-for spouses came and died, one being replaced by the other.

They both were good friends of mine. I never really thought too harshly about the consequences for their families until it happened to me too, other than once with her first mate, Peter. She simply bought these men away from their families—literally. She is a very wealthy woman, and that was her way of doing things. At first, it seemed harmless enough for I never knew any of their families, I thought.

I welcomed them as new mates and had incredibly good times developing a strong and active friendship as we sailed, golfed, and played tennis on the Canadian and American shores at our private clubs. If you sailed, did tennis seriously, and enjoyed more than you should have, then you were part of this crew, somehow, somewhere.

Today was another beautiful summer morning, and the day's activities hadn't even started, so it was to be smooth sailing ahead. We just always thought that that's how a summer morning should start.

Staring at the horizon gave me much tranquility and a sense of stability after a long drunken sailor's night out. I wasn't about to drop my eyes to the "crashing" surf against the rocks. A steady horizon and breathing the lake's ozone do wonders to cure a hangover. Each breath adds more life to the brain cells you just crushed. You have to choose your spot wisely though, for how close to the waters you can stay while awakening.

We always kept our eyes to the horizon to cure the inner alcohol tortures one usually encounters during wild summer recesses on this side of the lake. A distant, steady shoreline was always your best bet.

This morning, I have blissfully calm and gently rolling seas. The lake's deep-blue waters reflected crystal-clear images of wispy clouds in the sky. As with many of our past summer mornings, this was sunrise at its best, and my day has just begun. It offered me true richness in life. I could never replace this morning's smile with monetary value, although it is money you need to surround yourself within this blissful Canadian American sanctuary.

I used to sit like this—so content with my ex-wives.

We'd share emotions, holding a bond of eternity. Somehow now, I have the same tranquility with just myself. My dreams haven't changed, and my emotions still hope the same things. The wives just aren't here anymore. And it almost seems a shame not to share this again with someone special by my side, although I have grown to accept this temporary solitude without a pressuring need to "have to have" someone to share it with, at least for now.

If marital vows weren't meant to be kept, then one shouldn't have made them to begin with. It seems a waste of time to offer your heart and lose it in today's world. Marriage has become more of a lawyer's tool for employment and a spouse's way of collecting cash like in some reality game show *Divorced Today*.

MARK FRANCIS SCHWAB

I really don't know how much is "not worth that much" pain to pay for those shared emotions. It's a lawyer's game as you split your friends and money. Knowing less at that point is more. Just walk away and let the vultures and bottom feeders do it, controlling the hate that burns your mind, endlessly on sleepless nights.

I have kept my mind on the distant Buffalo skyline this morning.

There will be enough slurry for everyone after the weekend when we cross our beloved Peace Bridge and enter those buildings in a seemingly placid, distant city. Three of my exes are there somewhere. There will be no placid horizons from some twenty-seventh-floor window looking across the rooftops to these Canadian shoals.

My coffee was less than tepid now, and this personal sanctuary was quickly coming to its morning's end. I'll be back to the Lake Club, the summer homes, the boats and the summer-time residents soon, with such luxuries that can only be seen as inherited. I love most of my friends here, but love is a gift to give to one's self first, not used as a tool for buying another's love to have it for your own like what the spouse stealer has mastered as a science. Yet they are hand in hand, for the poor do not sip their morning coffee here on the Canadian shores.

The ex-wives loved this spot but have chosen other righteous, more expensive, exotic extravagances for placating their diversions. That's fine with me. Every now and then, one pops up at a social function of club-orchestrated charitable gifting. But these are tried and true friends whom I share these Canadian waters with every summer. It's a bond proven by time over many years.

There will be multiple female choices for new affection across the bridge in the city bars soon enough, so this sanctuary is revered yet not alone forever.

At least tonight, Nicholas Whinstner and I will be downing several rum drinks and shots, laughing at almost everything that we can think of after our sail later today, as well as anything we can remember from when we were kids growing up here at the Lake Club. Nicky and I have been friends since the beginning—kids wildly doing stuff that we needed parental okays for without having permission; and now, we are the ones shooting shots as the "adults at the bar" while our aged parents sit at the table like we used to.

Nick was a good sailor, probably one of the best here if not one of the most serious about the sport. He liked to look the part too, drinking some branded scotch at the helm of his sailing yacht. His clothes were everything you'd see in an advertisement, all the way to his crew neck sweater and captain's hat. He was a character all right. When he grew his tailored beard, he was the spitting image of any seafaring captain you've ever seen portrayed on television, right down to the square jawline. And he loved to grin for his challenged accomplishments, then and now.

Evening had arrived, and we all were back at the club.

"Quite the sailing day. Sorry I had to be in the city so long," Nick said with a downed shot glass on the bar, ordering for the both of us after this afternoon's sail.

"Had a good morning looking at the lake . . . You probably were on the bridge heading over," I said.

"Damn, I hadn't even gotten to the toll booths till eleven. To our next sail," Nick toasted in his grinning captain's way, securing in his mind our next leave-of-port call.

"To full sails *and* the wind!"

I pounded my drink down too and ordered another for both of us on my tab, with a nod of my head to the waiting, vested bartender. The club had a small bar, and he was serving only a few couples and us.

Glancing down the bar and back for Nick's attention, two younger women stood watching *two* drinking captains telling *drunken* stories. They made it obvious with a smile. They were members. They held each word we said, and Nick saw it too. Grinning to each other, we downed another shot. Nick long ago was married, and I wasn't sure if he'd follow through chasing new women for me like our younger days.

I gestured a toast to them and knew it best to leave that alone for now. One thing for sure, Nicholas would play the game until the last moment, making *my* game the real thing. It was expected of us, and this wasn't a public crowd in some Buffalo bar. Most were members and invited guests. Things had changed so much over the years with more members joining and coming of age like Nicky and me. A walk to the boathouse with a secret moon-lit trail for "nooky" was almost a long-forgotten late-teenage memory.

Nick loved to talk about the wind and the water under sail. He was always yelling "Trim the mizzen!" or "Prepare to come about!" Sailing was part of his blood, growing up since his first sailfish we'd use in the shallows of the bay back then. The boat was just big enough for two in fairly calm seas. Once in awhile, he'd take us into the depths of the lake outside of the bay. And once, we sailed around the point to the far dunes. I only went because I trusted him. His parents would have killed him if they knew. I was visiting for several weeks then, and my mother never would have known, neither would his.

Today, the club is like finding someone's wife (or mother) who was recently divorced or as the bachelor club-hawks who soar the shoreline in search of the newest member-prey to have.

But the spouse stealer is another matter altogether. They're searching without any care, no matter what the cost is or the marital status is of one who responds to them. There are so many unmarried people who I cannot understand why they would steal someone away from a whole family. How good is love anyway if you have to buy it? And what is that worth, especially since I've seen two of the spouse stealer's mates die from some degenerative cancers? A non-inheritance clause you'd bet she had; you could be sure of that.

During the weekdays, it was very peaceful here when most had to head back for city stuff. I'd walk the shores alone for hours and then have lunch with someone who never left during the day and, in some cases, for the summer. I would simply connect to my business editors through the Internet anyway. There, here—it made no difference other than having their stories before deadline.

Regardless, my new game plan was to date as many women as possible, finding that right woman again, and Nicky, as a true friend, was willing to help his old pal feel whole again. We both believed everyone should have a partner in life—going through it all—for we both thought of our lives as filled with adventures and companionship, and it was worth living it all.

# CHAPTER TWO

## *Retrospection*

I'VE COMMITTED MYSELF to the adventure again for that *someone* special, having all the family that comes with that, which in the eyes of God, is for better or worse, for richer or poorer, till death does "us" part. I just have to get out there more and chase potential mates now. Nicky always pushed me on that, although we weren't that close anymore after the second divorce. We'd sail once in a while and then drink at the bar. It's funny how you don't even know that you haven't been "out there" for the sanctuary and comfort you've created and become accustomed to.

I've done it before and can do it again. It just seems harder each time as we age and have less tolerance for all the dating bullshit. Shooting the shit with Nicky that night at the club put balls back into my pants, not to mention those attentive "members" at the end of the bar that night! Those remembrances of a "good walk to the boathouse" do one wonders for summoning the courage you've once experienced, regardless of how many years ago you felt so fearless.

At least I'm positive about starting this game, having no sack of negatively charged rocks I've dragged along after my last divorce. And if negatives appear, the goodness in my soul takes over that battle of depression, for with every negative comes a positive. It's chemistry, and that is science; then, the science of marriage could work again: protons and neutrons joining themselves among the ice in our glasses rather than self-destructing.

Most everyone goes for the better, for we try to "come about" as sailors tacking the seas. We simply are seeking forgiveness within the winds for all behavior, hoping that we've turned on the right tack, pressing onward toward the finish line.

I began to meet several new people, replacing those old friends after signing my divorce papers. Sadly, we lose so many at once once the deal is done. The thought of starting a new list of "lovers" to eventually choose *one* from who could be the one was actually exciting me. That feeling, the strength and the drive to start over, is one of the great moments in life, for there is nothing more enlightening than sharing happiness with a smile just to see theirs. My void from the divorce and the "lost family" is rarely seen in the mirror anymore from a glaring summer hangover. I'd need a good pinching if the Canadian shoals and Lake Erie's ozone-filled air didn't awaken me each day!

Marriage has a meaning we all want: to have and hold a constant constitution that is never to change, ever! Marriage is supposed to give you that in God's contract or, in this case, the State of New York.

That's why *they* make it permanent for the rest of your life. There's no pretending saying those words and going through the motions. For me, on both times, I never wanted that emotion to end, ever. You work together to fill your souls with love, trust and happiness and just fix the other stuff. Trying to live on only one side—a selfish side, of course—just wastes time, and finally the bill comes due, for it always does, as Hemingway once wrote. Any delaying of its presentation adds only to more confusion and guilt.

I'm not saying that all feeling is gone after a long marriage, for I still have an emotional side for one who will never die or leave me.

But there's an incredible sickness a spouse stealer can inflict on so many without notice. It's something that kills all rational thought, temporarily—something that strikes a real nerve like buying someone away from their family, using sickening sums of money to make them forget their historic pasts and then making them become content in a new world of corrupt indifference. Stealing for instant gratification is the devil's work and nothing less. For most of us, finding the right one takes great time, effort and understanding. A partnership is a work of art—elusive, yes, yet requiring thoughtful role playing, determination and commitment to keep it moving forward. Those first days of being in love, when you kiss for hours, gaze into eyes that reflect your own emotions and lust for touching and sharing sexual pleasures, need great care to preserve them throughout time together, . . . and it ages quickly in front of your eyes, and you don't even see it—the tree for the forest.

My divorces happened with contemptuous speed, but then add in those shylock's time, who are the only ones that really say it's over, on paper. Divorce is less real, in my opinion, when on paper, although we read every damn word, forcing ourselves through it, sometimes with an almost audible vengeance, if not with a few figurative gestures.

There have been several women I've dated so far—some good and some not so good: they are good looking, fair looking, slender, not so slender and a complete array of beautiful and not-so-beautiful breasts. I'm a breast man. Small, perky and pointing nipples that grow hard in good foreplay with the exciting meetings of the minds are it! It's the banana joke of men! You can always tell when we're happy to see you.

Sex can seem to be everything, but it's not—honestly.

Men sometimes can only think with their dicks. If the girl is not for you, it's just smarter not wasting anyone's time, especially hers. Having someone become heartbroken and disappointed just doesn't cut it, so "move on" as Yul Brenner said in the *Magnificent Seven*. Time is life, and the love, money and effort, wasted or not, are still all mine. We move on. We have to keep our faith for our sanity.

But a real spouse stealer can never change their cheating ways. I've seen it, saw their tactics and tried to put blinders on, leaving them to their own disrespectful ways. You can't take them seriously, other than simply being devoid of their actions.

"For better or worse, till death do you part?" I do remember saying yes to that, but can the spouse stealer? You can never see it coming is all I can say!

That kind of money ruins people, and she's a class act. I hate having blinders on in complacency, yet that's exactly what I thought that keeps me able to safely tack the seas ahead then.

The marriage/divorce rate is roughly 50/50 or slightly more so on one side; either way, that's the current rate! There's fault on all sides, including "those people" who shouldn't have been involved in the first place but stuck their dripping noses where it shouldn't have been in the first place.

Why in hell do people try to hurt the ones they've loved for so long during their divorces? And why do "these friends" choose a side and consciously fuel the fire with speculative and hate-filled emotions? "Wait till I make him hit rock bottom," my ex said to my mother. It was a freak'n game to her! What a shit. I was hanging on, hoping to keep the house that she secretly secured for herself. Damn those blinders to keep us running in a straight line! I know my first wife put my dog to sleep, for I never saw him again, nobody did. That was the toughest part: not knowing where, how or what became of that old lovable Airedale. He vanished one day while I was on a business trip. It wasn't my home anymore either, for she moved out all my things, including the dog, and changed the locks before I arrived home. Everything mine was gone from my house! That feeling stays with me today. Was that rock bottom? Is that the meaning of fucking one over till it hurts? The message is embedded in my mind about how sick some people can be. You have to just walk away. It was overkill and one sick way of getting a rise for emphasis, is all I can say.

There's another hot spot in divorce: the children, the nieces, the nephews, the cousins and in-laws. The spouse stealer's *first stolen* had two kids! All and any feelings changed from happiness to distain for my wife regarding them. Why parents use their children as objects in some imaginary chess game; moving them forward and back to "advantage" their outcome is sinful and unchristian.

The messages are so mixed to the kids; it's no wonder they repeat things: swear words or words simply used to provoke attention. It gives a whole new meaning to potty training. If loving mates only knew what they just played in their selfish minds, they'd see checkmate for both sides. I never had any children of my own from either marriage. But I've been close enough to the nieces and the nephews that I always thought family meant forever—no matter what nor how mad or long it takes to come back to mutual understanding. In-laws too become only a temporary family.

Funny how your councilor always makes believe that the divorce decree from the judge's ruling can go either way. These jurist doctorates always say, "You never know who the judge is . . . It could go either way . . . It depends who the judge is." Isn't that the truth? But those briefcase-carrying asses afford their country clubs and Ferraris on us, getting paid regardless of who wins or loses! Then, they have drinks and joke together as if nothing happened, only counted work. Just pay the bill. "Shylocks!" Shakespeare certainly depicted the truth for our pound of flesh.

If only we knew better not to react like Pavlov's dogs when we're weak and vulnerable in such unbelievable situations.

Belief in God is best, at least for me, for that belief can certainly help with lessening the emotional trauma and healing. When that guy in the black robe, high up behind a wooden edifice, swings his gavel, his hammer is final. Justice? Supposedly. The only winners are the lawyers with their pound of flesh filling their pockets. Shylocks and gavel wielders—a bad nightmare for marriage, especially for those with children. It is instant gratification or instant hell when you're adjourned.

We should just kill all spouse stealers who can be identified on site. Simply look for their money and newest of everything, especially their mate! Or put your blinders on and walk away. Everyone should take a good walk in the woods and leave their golf clubs home!

In a Woody Allen movie where he walks up to a so-happily-appearing couple and asks how they do it, "I'm stupid," she said, and he continued, "I'm very shallow."

Gilded people make it look so easy after they stick their toes in the water, as Mark Twain once jokingly said, "If I have to give up one of wine, women or song, I guess I'll give up singing!" How true for the spouse stealer.

I'm burning bridges so much less as getting older, putting that hell behind us as best as possible. For me, I'm in a web of somewhat steamy debauchery now as I search for someone by the numbers, and so the game is on hoping that one will rise above the rest.

# CHAPTER THREE

# *Olympic Games*

I WAS BACK in the city early, and the summer was almost over for the year. The snow would fall soon, relentlessly for several months with later mounds of black ice lining the highways caused by all the salt, sand and gravel they'd used. Summer on the lake would be a long-awaited next season.

The fall in Buffalo for me was the time for nightlife on Elmwood Avenue. There were at least half a dozen bars we frequented back in the city, meeting our friends and any potential mates, but then again, there were a few bars on Hertle Avenue for the more bohemian culture. Elmwood was it though. Most upscale and blue bloods stayed in this geographic corner of Buffalo as we took care of business.

The leaves were beginning to blow across dampened streets, and I was wearing a tan barracuda jacket instead of my usual sports coat or suit. It was a colder early fall night in Buffalo. I looked at the trees and knew that the rest of the leaves would be down within the month. If we had an extended fall, which is good for living on this side of the lake, we would have to pay dearly for it if the lake didn't freeze sooner into winter.

I crossed the street and went into No Names as we called it. The bar had no name, just a number in a massive wall of windows lining the sidewalk. You could see the crowd, if there was one. Tonight, the crowd wasn't thick and was workable. Sometimes you couldn't even move, but tonight I walked right in. I was on a mission to find another mate, so I looked to all eyes open.

A leggy, good-looking blonde was standing by herself at the neon-lighted brass dance rail. She had an air about her that denoted a well-mannered, solid upbringing. Her dress was quite exquisite, having the latest color schemes: light grey with white accents, and wearing an accenting scarf, which were the colors this year, dyed suede vest and pants. She filled her persona with curved hips and a long neckline. She hand no rings on her fingers, only matching silver earrings, necklace and bracelet. It was a very classic look, and she wore it well. Her skin was smooth and blemish-free, and her eyes were a deep blue. She wore make-up that could have been styled for a runway model, not heavy but with perfect rosy hues across her cheekbones. Pink gloss accented her lips. No one could have asked for more, other than being able to start up some conversation with her.

"What am I doing, able to talk to you . . . alone at the rail . . . without company?"

"Sorry, I'm with my boyfriend."

"Where in hell is he, leaving *you* alone?"

"Talking to those girls at the bar."

I'm Jonathon," I said, holding my hand out for a cordial recognition.

"Elizabeth."

As we talked, I saw that one could still maneuver to the bar for a cocktail. Elizabeth stood with an empty glass, patiently watching her boyfriend flirt with those girls. I asked the "question" that would allow our encounter to continue.

"Buy you a drink?"

"Yes, why not. White wine, please."

With drinks in hand, I walked back looking at her sheer eloquence and beauty.

"What's with being against the rail Lizzy?"

"Just standing away from the crowd at the bar."

"Yes, it's starting to be a bit of a cattle call in here. Sure you're with that guy?"

"I am," she replied, "I don't know what he's doing over there."

MARK FRANCIS SCHWAB

I could see a slightly stocky older man talking to two girls half his age and half as good-looking as Elizabeth. They looked pudgy in my eyes. And *he* reminded me of an old French turtle. His shoulders were somewhat rounded in his well-tailored suit, and his neck had an aged sagging under the chin. He had an air of sophistication and refinement to him but was definitely older than Elizabeth too.

"They're not even cute. Mind if I stand and chat for a bit?"

"All right, he doesn't seem to be coming back right away," she said, half smiling.

You could tell she wanted someone friendly to talk with and didn't like standing alone at the rail, and damn if I wasn't here searching for someone special at this numbered meat rack. Getting her number was the key, for it is later, after the first meeting, that you become better friends.

"Wish I knew a better way," I said.

"What's that?" she lifted her face, looking straight into my eyes.

Thank god, the music and the noise were loud enough that she didn't quite hear me. And what a stupid statement I just made!

"This place is so crowded," I said quickly. "You always have to go to crowded bars to have fun."

"Yes, it appears that way."

"I'm glad . . . ever married?"

"Yes, once a long time ago."

"Good 'cause you're damn good-looking and shouldn't be standing alone . . . *At the rail*. I'm glad I stopped."

It was right in there in front of me, with the pitch, but it came out so naturally that I felt myself meaning all of it, even the pickup lines.

"So . . . what do you do?" asking her the next "typical" question.

"Financial broker." She said it with pride and an air of confidence. I could hardly wait to spew mine.

"I'm a writer."

"*Really?*" she asked inquisitively.

A writer. That always gets them for some reason, for what's a writer other than a romantic name for the unknown? It's as if there's a deep mystery hidden within our souls waiting to expound emotional rhetoric with contemporary conjecture and meaning for all. I'm an industrial writer for manufacturing publications for god's sake, but I dabble with poetry for the fun. "I like to start a poem just to see if I can get out" Robert Frost once wrote.

"Yep, I write industrial stories on machines and how they work—things like that."

"Where?"

I saw it coming, my time to indulge a self-descriptive importance and a command on our topics.

"Trade journals and scientific magazines. I've been doing it for years. It's freelance but very successful."

I wouldn't pull the poetry bullshit out yet. Hell, I'll blow my proverbial cover, not that I have one. Technical writing can be the most boring task in the world to many, but I actually like knowing how everything works. I describe how that industrial shit is made, operates, and how those machines changed our lives. I love it—analyzing the testing, being on the plant floors and understanding the applications and the usage around the world.

"Yep, trade journals," I could only say. "It's extremely technical, *boring stuff*, but I like it."

"Like what?"

"It's all manufacturing companies, engines, farm machines, injection molding, . . . stuff like that. So what about you?"

It was small talk, but it was going well enough—no lulls—especially since her friend didn't care what she was doing or with whom.

"Really . . . I trade for my clients . . . manage their account at our firm. I've been there for over twenty years," she said.

"No shit, how'd you get into trading?"

Dumb, but I never did have much of a portfolio and knew little about what stocks to buy. I used a broker a few times and never cared much for their commissions or their recommended picks. His stocks usually fell in value but he got paid anyway, buying and selling just like the attorneys getting their pound of flesh no matter what.

"Money—it all came down to money. I like the job, but it's the money," she said.

"I love my job too . . . It pays pretty well."

Comparing jobs and money seemed more about the money and less about the love for the process. I was at the top-end scale on mine, and I wouldn't change a damn thing for any job, certainly not chasing money for commission. It's been my freelance enterprise for as long as I can remember—my love of writing for a living.

"I hate it when it comes to that . . . money or happiness. We should all stay in our first-loved professions . . . if you love your work that much," I said defending us truly gratified workers.

It all comes down to personal satisfaction on "how much is enough." The movie *Wall Street* flashed in my mind when Bud Fox asked that infamous question to Gordon Gecko. I'm not on commission and never will be.

And what the fuck did I just say to her anyway? How out there and esoteric without transitions our conversation! Where was my conjunctive statement about love of a chosen vocation? *In written sentences, yes I know.* But I certainly defined life as one that "money won't ever equal love and happiness."

We talked for an hour, only to reveal that she was semi-living with the man at the bar. She had her own apartment, but he was still there somewhere, off to some other side, chewing the fat with podgy girls, not paying attention. She was half living there at his home. Apparently, he was some rich type with tons of money.

The crowd was moving upon us, and I felt almost as if I was babysitting for her unatentative, turtle-looking boyfriend. He was a strangely featured man, being very well dressed, with aging features and skin like a sea turtle. It all was good though, for his preoccupation and forgotten "belle of the ball" was with me, at least for the moment, knee-deep in conversation of all kinds. Once, we looked into each other's eyes for a bit of crowding security, and she momentarily did not care what the French turtle was doing. In fact, she seemed to relish our lengthy conversation! A much younger man, I might add. And god, was she a "standout" in the crowd.

Simply, it was pleasurable conversation. She gave me her number with some reluctance, but after looking across the bar once more, she thought why not? I made her feel like a lady and with a true interest in what she had to say.

I thought not to let this darling go and kept talking but knew I must take my cue once I had the toughest part out of the way, a number on a napkin. And that's all I wanted from this stellar beauty right now—her number to call at a later date. You could tell she shared feelings of new friendship as did I. How else does a "taken" woman talk so much and give an opportunity to continue other moments by giving up her number? It wasn't anything about sex at this point that stimulated me—it was an emotional compatibility between two people sharing thoughts. And she was damn beautiful.

What a loser her boyfriend was not to see the light, missing the point that she was one great lady slipping from his world. He was a loser not to hold something he so obviously had in his hands, his life and future. If love is blind, this guy is deaf, dumb, *and* blind. He takes the cake. You never let someone like this go without major efforts to keep them, if you can have them. And she was upfront about a lot of the "living situation" she shared. At first, that really blew my mind but made it all the more challenging in my quest for "real" love again.

I was the single one here, and this was our first meeting. Love pulls no punches after you are left alone seeking someone special. And alone is not the name of this game now. Not if I can help it. Maybe Lizzy's boyfriend will be the one alone, for I am to call with her blessings. One thing for sure, I am not a "spouse stealer" with Lizzy.

Statistically, the numbers are counted when the gavel-swinging judge ends legal life together. Those robe wearers have the power to accept the lawyer's presentation, taking it from a great fabric of harmonious love into single threads. Only the strongest love is greater than the printed word or a wooden gavel. Thank god Lizzy wasn't married to this guy!

"It was most interesting and enjoyable talking with you," Elizabeth said.

I nodded with a smile, knowing we both thought it might be greener on the other side. I gave her my card.

"Call me. I'd love to hear from you . . . when you can," she said.

That's how it all started—talking about everything, including the void of her boyfriend's attention. I had her number and the invitation to call her.

I can't help thinking: searching for a good woman is an acceptable affair but over self-indulgence is another thing. I admit there is a fine line in the heat of battle, but there *is* a line that must be communicated with everyone from the start of any sexual endeavors. Before that, it's all bullshit, and each side has the right of passage, literally. That's that. I had taken at least three "numbered" napkins that evening and felt completely talked out with no real player, with mostly forgettable faces except for Elizabeth's. I needed to go home.

Looking at all the names and numbers I had collected over the last few weeks, I put hers in my desk drawer too. Everything was written on the back of napkins, business cards or strips of paper tablecloth, anything you could write on. I thought I could remember most every detail for whose number went to whose faces. I simply lost myself in mixed memories, stacking them in a rubber-banded stack. Elizabeth was filed on top, and she was to be mine, somehow. I'll have to make some calls soon.

## Games in Between

There were now five or six good women to think about it. Most have some little note or marking of recognizable identification on their napkin, small pieces of torn paper tablecloth or cards that holds their number. Good or bad. Not everyone was active or wanted active pursuit, but many wanted to be in the game. I never wasted time calling the best ones first.

Elizabeth wasn't home when I called, but Jeannie was always available. Jeannie was becoming a main stay, at least for now, and she knows of the others in the drawer, so I was being honest with her. She really didn't seem to mind the thought at all.

She had dark-brown shoulder-length hair that was always scented with some fabulous fragrant, perky little breasts and incredible runner's legs. She dressed rather conservatively without panache and without any jewelry. Her style was more like fresh preppie school clothes that never aged. They were always fresh and dry cleaned.

We started right into having sex on our first date, and it was now getting to be fabulous—the kind any single man would kill for, live for. The activities, the sex and the shared intoxicating adventures were all there. Jeannie was worth keeping high up on the list's pack.

You can't be married and have this much fun, ever, for many wives wouldn't or couldn't be so "experimental," but I wasn't going to think about that now. It's not in my vocabulary to be married at this stage of the game. Marriage was then, and this is now: placating debauchery, looking. I'm living for the day, for the plan and, damn it, for the pleasure too.

And I wasn't going to make the mistake of taking any of them for granted either, for each and every one of these beautiful women in the drawer had their own personality. They have their own rights for passage too. And if I'm the one they want to sail with, well, they just booked a fucking good captain. I'm not on any women's schedule to be pushed into love again right now. When you become this happy in the garden, only you can choose what fruit to taste and grow upon harvesting, for it's my garden. This was my moment of rebirth, answering the echoes from the abyss left behind me, and I'm not afraid to test these waters once again.

Jeannie and I thought of our sex as a kind of a secret club with hidden kinky secrets done with each other—things that one never really discusses but just does as they happen. We were making it up as we went along. I so pity those who have never had it like this before they die. Once experienced, there's no forgetting—maybe no return for some, for it was and is one or the greatest of feelings.

Sex will make or break a marriage. It's that simple. Maybe not in the beginning, but it will in the end. When you've aged further and want what wasn't there to begin with, knowing that it's simply not going to be there later, a marriage will end. Jeannie and I couldn't care less about commitments other than when we were going to do it next.

If you're married and can't get "it," like the famous question "Depends on what is, is . . . ?" William Jefferson, a.k.a. Bill, Clinton would have asked, and then you're shit out of luck, unless you cheat, and we all know where cheating gets you. And there are all kinds of cheating, not just sex cheating. Look in the mirror and ask yourself what kinds you think there are. Nobody's free from everything considered cheating like "white" lying, so don't confuse cheating with the least form of cheating. They're one and the same. Jeannie and I were honest with each other from the start.

Elizabeth still hadn't returned any of my calls and with my darling, Jeannie, there wasn't a need for a lot of organizing, at least for talking about it. She was always ready, and we screwed every time we were together. We did spend some time talking, but after any date activity, we'd jump into bed. She's a nurse, and we didn't talk about that either. She's a "pan handler," helping people go in their beds, which probably is why water sports fascinated her so much.

We always took long country drives, drinking beer on the back mountainous roads and singing to the old Doobie Brothers. We loved *Taking It to the Streets*. Michael McDonald's voice was smooth as silk. When we returned, it was right up to the bedroom and living out the erotic behavior we thought about on our drives. We weren't sharing any family or friends, just fun times and sex. Our relationship was definitely not complicated, at least not in the beginning.

We just loved that male/female single stuff not to be challenged—no ties, no marriage plans. We didn't need the pressures of making commitments, especially any wrong ones. After all, that's the whole point of what I'm experiencing here. Now's my time to sample the waters, see and smell the blossoms—every damn one of them. I'm not going

MARK FRANCIS SCHWAB

to choose too quickly again, although I know from prior experiences that when on this path, someone will push for it soon enough. The sex thing has to work before love though; otherwise, it would later bite me on the ass like a bad dog.

Jeannie was giving me so much joy being such a younger, athletic and kinky women. I could almost call her "girl" for how she behaves and tries sexually anything we think of. She's around twenty-six, knows what she wants, wild and experimental. We were doing it almost daily. And at my age, that's pushing the envelope!

One night, I was surprised to hear her say, "More, give me more—"

"What? You want me to say more dirty things? Real dirty? I said, dropping my head, looking into her eyes with raised eyebrows as if I had reading glasses on.

I could feel my penis grow to the stiffest I've felt that evening. She did too, literally.

"Anything . . . everything you want," Jeannie said squeezing my balls, as only a nurse knows how much pressure before total pain.

After that, going out for dinner wasn't an option. We always ordered pizza and things, and rented a movie from pay-for-view that cable TV was now offering. The sheets were always wet with our sweat, and that suited us both.

For tomorrow, we planned an afternoon drive, knowing that when we return, we are going to do it again, but we loved doing our spontaneous country drive destinations first. They were as adventuresome as our sex.

The car was packed as we were heading down suburban roads to the thruway which would take us to the back country. We loved the visual stuff on the rural backroads—things like cows in a pasture, the rising of flat land into foothills, and the semi-deserted unevenly paved roads where only locals lived—and our time singing to the music. We knew or felt our dreams would not include each other later in life, but we shared them as one for the time being.

"What do you want to hear?" I ask Jeannie as I was down-shifting for a bend in the road, knowing full well that she'll listen to my Michael McDonald imitations.

"McDonald?"

"Of course, darling girl, what else?" I said putting my arm around her shoulder.

I grabbed a CD from my holder, not knowing what it was going to be like Russian roulette. Stills & Nash or KC and the Sunshine Band? I had no idea, just guesses.

I pulled out John Baldry . . . "Going Up North To Get My Hambone Boiled!" We laughed and I gave her the holder to choose whatever she wanted to hear.

"Want a beer?" she asked.

"Not till we get off the thruway at least . . . I brought some smoke too."

"You keep me happy . . . I like that."

"What pleases my girl, pleases me," I gave her a quick kiss on her cheek.

"That's what I love best about you . . . pleasing me first—always . . . so satisfying."

"Always liking the women to orgasm first. No point without it," I smiled.

We just hit the thruway exit, and everything is good today for sure. Nothing like all the positive thoughts to start things out.

"Are you ready?" She was already reaching into the bag behind the seat for a beer. She handed me mine and opened one too.

"Got 'em cold, don't you?"

"Only way—warm beer sucks."

"I know . . . but you like warm water."

"Damn, darling, it's your warm water."

I downed the first beer in several large gulps. She cracked another and put my empty in the pack. We'd always dumped the empties on any pit stops in case we got stopped by the cops. No empties, no apparent crime. No slurred words either, if you could help it, of course.

"Gonna be a good day, I can see," she said with a bit of spirit.

"Yep, I'm totally game for *all* of it."

She smiled at me so sadistically my hard-on was showing through my pants.

"Whoa, the little boy's growing now!" she said looking at me, reaching over and gripping me hard, which just made it seem harder.

"You get me too horny sometimes."

"That's why I like it. I felt that move!" she said.

"Growing's a wonderful thing," I said, thinking of what my orgasm does for her.

We had turned onto the backroads, having left the exit almost unknowingly like a horse instinctively running to water knowing the

MARK FRANCIS SCHWAB

way. It was a blue sky, and the smell of hay mowing in country fields was everywhere. I do love the countryside.

"There's a crazy hillbilly bar up here. Shall we have a shot with the locals?"

"Yes! Let's do it," she said turning her head to me.

I threw the shift into third gear to slow down for the upcoming curve and turned the music up, holding the wheel tightly with one hand, and grabbing her tit with the other as we came into the straight away. I love this little sports car.

We pulled into the graveled lot with a small yellowish block building and a lit Budweiser sign in its single, little window. There were only a few cars and an old Harley parked in front.

"Locals, you can be sure. Let's have a couple and split when we get the look. Got it?" I said.

"Done. Let's just fuck'em a little. No major shit, just tease 'em and out."

"You got it."

"A few shots and we're gone, just don't get carried away . . . You know you," she said.

"Cool as a cucumber."

We were going to toy with these locals all the way through this pit stop. Using her nips pointing through her braless shirt, shots and beers, maybe a game of pool and my money on the bar as the plan.

Everyone, five or seven maybe, glared at us as we entered their world from the outside. The barroom was darkened in every corner. There were smoke-filled lights over the bar, pool table and surrounding the jukebox's lit selections.

It was their domain, and they sized up a hot female like coyotes wanting there next meal. Jeannie's outfit made them drool, as she had on short-cut jean shorts and a tank top exposing just a touch of stomach and belly button and her nipples popping almost as see-through. Their mouths were open with wildly imagined lust, especially when she ordered a shot of whiskey and beer chaser for us.

I'm never sure what these hillbillies think, drinking most of the day in their local bars, and now with a chick giving her superior glances to them with a simple smile! I am sure the place loves my money too. New money to them always opens their eyes, good or bad.

"Make that a Seagrams Seven with Canadian beer," I said loud enough to the bartender. You could tell they instantly hated me and wished for her. It was in their eyes. I saw it and couldn't resist making mine a double shot. It at least let these hillbillies know that we partied too somewhere across their border

"Let's buy the bar a round too," I said.

That always breaks the ice when a stranger buys a round, drinking worthlessly in their unpaved sanctuary. I never buy just one if the crowd is small enough, with *their* prices, so I ordered another round for after that too on my tab. I knew that would placate and keep them in order for a while.

"The music, darling," I said.

"Give me a five so it plays till we leave."

"Done, baby girl. Let's keep 'em happy and somewhat normal. *All* eyes are on *those* nips!" I said pointing a finger, resting my hand against my chest so not to be seen.

Jeannie changed the music from country-crying to rock-and-roll. She also put quarters down on the table, won the game, changing it to doubles to include me, and one more of them. Jeannie showed her tight calves and butt stretching across the table as she shot that first game, and I told a few very dirty jokes to continue placating their obvious obsessions. I was saddened a little about how much these farm folks loved animal jokes. They'll be talking about us for the rest of their lives.

We left within the hour, for they wanted more than just shots of whiskey and a game of pool. We wanted what the open road had waiting around the bend, although this was a good and a worthy stop; however, we were early into the trip and greater adventures lay ahead.

We dusted the parking lot, strapped in the buckets as I popped the clutch.

"That was so good . . . what fun doing that. We always do it *so* right . . . out like this, *I love it!*" she said with a big grin and victory-clinched fists.

"What else can we expect . . . fuck'en with local yokels in their place . . . us being such fuck'en outsiders buying their drinks? We are their *free memories* for life," I said.

"Other than their cattle and children. Damn, think of their children . . . and wives for Christ's sake," she said shaking her head lightly.

"Yeh, that too . . . scary . . . we'll never see them again and *can't do a damn thing* for 'em anyway."

"You're so sad. That Bill guy was cute. I liked him."

"Woulda, coulda, shoulda—"

"I'm here, babe," Jeannie said with affectionate eyes.

"Billybob-boy just smiled . . . thinking of what could be if ever in your bed . . . do these people actually think? That's why we take these drives . . . to forget the stress."

Bill was a good-looking farm boy lost in cow or horse-shit, but he liked Jeannie, as she controlled all of them. You could tell he was a proud boy from some large family farm. Jeannie seems to take a conciliatory fancy to them though, but not when in the city. She might have family somewhere like this that made her power so great among them. Her nips certainly didn't hurt. But this was *our* adventure; otherwise, we could just as easily watch the movie *Deliverance*, drinking our beers.

"Another?" she said already reaching for two more.

"Damn right, I'm ready. Ready to fuck you by some stream right now."

"*Good . . . let's do it.*" She grinned lifting her brow, eyeing her kinkiness into mine.

"I got'a piss like a race horse after all that beer," I said.

"Me too."

After a few miles I pulled over next to a small bridge crossing a creek bed with a small stand of trees that would give us cover.

I love watching chicks piss in the outdoors. This was hardly the woods though. A slight down slope with a few trees to hide naked truth from passing cars, not that anyone driving on this backroad would think to look for anything other than making the next drunken curve. Little did they know. We went in front of each other. It's good to have a girl that can piss outside right in front of you and not give a shit.

"Enjoying this, aren't you?"

"Yes, I do—it's way too cool. I love watching you flow—"

As she squatted, it streamed far out in front of her, so what the fuck was Freud saying about "Man's supremacy to Woman because they couldn't piss out the campfire" for? Jeannie can shoot just as far as I can within the right position and that could douse a good campfire. We do have the angling-advantage though.

"Bet you can't spell your name in the snow," I said.

"No, but I can hit your face on my back, so stand still."

"Later, we haven't the cover!" I placated her while doing "*the* double shake" to show I was playing along with her.

Back in the car, we took several more curving country roads now leading home. The sun was sharply from the west and requiring sunglasses. Our heading was north by northwest toward the city and parallel to Lake Erie. We always played rockstar when wearing our shades in the sports car.

"We need to do one of our drive-thrus for beer and wine for later," I said.

Everything was now gone from the cooler except a few warm ones. We always mapped in our minds where the next "stops" were for bathrooms and "cold ones" as we neared the city. After reaching the house, we cracked open two more cold beers, set the wine in the freezer, and headed up to my room. I was grabbing everything on her that I could going up the stairs. I love her pointed, braless nipples showing through her shirt like that. Jeannie's were so young and perky, and she knew it turned me on.

She's stripped off her top as we got near the bed. I dropped my pants, pointing my dick at her, and pushed her back onto the bed, pulling her now unbuckled pants and underwear off together.

What more can I say about her in the raw like this, fresh from our drive and straight into bed without any wash-ups? She was always clean . . . always. There's little smell on her other than our mingling sweat. It takes a woman to know her body that well to be so clean after a day's adventures like we just had. With most others, we'd make sure to the showers first. But Jeannie never smelled of anything unhealthy, and I loved that about her.

She was on me, and the warm water bottle with the spout up was on the bed's ledge. She loved me squirting her with warm water.

"*Looking pleased!* I can see your eyes," I said.

"Totally . . . ready," she said as I started squirting her with the water before we engaged in full intercourse and our lengthy enjoyable extra pleasures.

"Are you satisfied with that? Can't say another damn thing then lay here," I said, having orgasm-ed.

"You're breathing very hard."

"You know us older men," I said raising an eyebrow, trying to look smarter and younger.

I rolled over on my back, and she was on top of me in a flash. I didn't give a shit if the sheets and towels were wet or not. I'd worry about all that later, for she was in control and there was no stopping her from her desires. She was the right choice, for both of us, at least at this time: fabulously sensual and warmer than a bath without submerging yourself—hot and wild. I masturbated to ejaculation just as she did. That's my Jeannie, kinky as all hells get out.

She was ready again, like she always was. I could tell just by looking into her eyes as her leg was rubbing mine. I wasn't ready for anything other than hugs and kisses. I left it at that, for any more excitement and I should have died of a heart attack for as much as I am playing . . . with her and myself. I was near total hyperventilation. Everything was warm, wet and lengthy. She rolled over on and we stared at the ceiling fan with thoughts of ecstasy. Our sex was it—pure nympho-stuff wanted and done by both of us. And it was going further into sexual desires than ever before. It was a dare! She loved every drop to fuel her orgasms and wasn't this what it was all about, pleasing organisms? Certainly not marriage at this stage of the game.

She wasn't from the city or surrounding suburbs but from some small town. Her family lived somewhere deep in the Midwest. She moved to Buffalo to escape the fields of corn and small-town living, not that she lived on the farms, just in the rural towns. There was her, her mother and her sister who was younger in the immediate family. Her parents were divorced, and she didn't speak of her father at all. Nobody was close from what I could gather, and I wasn't going to interrupt our fun for those answers. Sad but how strong some people's desires are acted out when so estranged from their families. I know the feeling. I'm from an estranged family too, having put much of those thoughts aside. It is hard to want something you cannot have like a normal family, one that never leaves you, ever. Sadly, that's become the ideal, not the norm. It happens sooner or later to most of us, and Jeannie was in a much worse boat than I for having less of a family to see on holidays. Once you've reached dealing with your estranged family, there is no way back unless you start one of your own. No past, no history to recall, just the future for moving forward. Jeannie and I have something—something that will always be shared and remembered.

I do love Jeannie for her toughness and sheer beauty, as young as she was to me. She is a strong, good-looking woman, a professional and damn sexual. People like us just survive the estranged pain, put it away and move into some muted happiness for a while. We aren't deprived of the joys in life, but rather we push the envelope that can scare way too many people. Yet our overindulgence is much wanted by those who don't or can't ever dare what we're doing. It is with past pain that Jeannie and I enjoy the pleasures we share now. We just made it look easy like the painted models in Henry James' story "The Real Thing." It was smiles and fun all the time. The stories we'd tell others were always met with "Are you making this up?" Shit, who can make up such things as we've done? They're just too far out there *not* to be true—like our sex! Who the fuck really goes that far with country drives, peeing by streams, laughing at drunken cowboys and coming home to such wild debauchery as a plan? There's no lying, cheating or stealing here . . . for what's the freak'en point of having such unabashed sex together? We both knew you couldn't get here unless you paid for it somehow! To me, there's always sunshine when she's here, and sometimes when she's not just thinking about her. We simply went on with our plans to plan nothing and then start again on another day. Just like today. We were in sync with a sort of love to share everything, no matter what it was. We felt as some strange kind of family together: a trusting unity, sharing our thoughts and desires.

"I have a girlfriend who wants to have sex with me," Jeannie said as we still laid on the bed. I looked to the ceiling in another planned ecstasy for what she just said.

"Really? Can we do *this all together?*"

"Don't know if she'll do that—" she lingered in mid sentence, moving her eyes to me with a half smile on her face.

"Come on, she'll do it if we do it . . . you think?"

"I'll ask her . . . This may be too wild, but I've been thinking about it for a while now . . . She acts like she wants to."

I could have been drooling like those hillbillies in the bar as almost speechless.

"When are you seeing me next? Aren't we going somewhere . . . maybe?" she said putting her arm across my chest.

"Soon," I said, "very soon."

We got dressed, straightened up the bed and then I walked her to her car, giving her a big kiss good-bye. My thoughts were racing. Could I have this new experience too? What about the several "natural wonders" still on those numbered napkins in my drawer? All different and magnificent in their own right. And there's still Lizzy to think about. What a prize she'd make!

This made it even harder than ever to think about putting Jeannie back in the drawer for another name. But the next one could be even better, maybe the one. Jeannie's a great gal, but I wasn't going to marry her, and she knew that. She knows she's not the only one in the drawer too. It's a sea of mermaids out there, and I was trolling.

I walked into the house and truly hoped Jeannie can find *herself* a plan, like I have, to build herself a family again.

She was still the beginning of this dating game—a damn good beginning, so no prisoners or commitments again until ready. What the tides and the stars are telling me at this point, I don't have a fucking clue yet. "That's the way it is"—thanks Walter Cronkite. It never lasts with sex as the primary point for the relationship, but it all was damn good: always seeming too short near the end, but then again, sometimes being too long from the start. Being single again meant that I didn't have to keep them all straight, just able to remember their faces, names and numbers—and their desires.

# CHAPTER FOUR

# *Choices or Triumphs*

I T WAS ALL there in the desk drawer, with so many already sampled to feel that I'm moving forward, and not sitting home alone like I used to so often in retrospection and lack of all desire to socialize since that last divorce.

Where to go and who should be called next? It really didn't matter to ask which was better, smarter or sexier; it became simply who was available. What other reasons than *doing* the shortness of breath from the heat of desire? It was so good to love so much and so many without the recourses. I am single and my own man until I find *the love in life* again, so there are no constraints early in this game.

I found Tiffany's number. "Toufutie, Toufutie, where are you when I needed you?" as I called her—you know, the movie with Kurt Russell and Goldie Hawn titled *Overboard.* The drunken snob just wants women in his stateroom and all over the floor of his boat since the madam was out. In reality, I was not crying the question into a seashell, for Tiffany was on for today's ride and evening play.

So I renamed her napkin Toufutie instead of Tiffany as *the* secret of the drawer to get into her drawers! When I told her, she loved the nickname too, for she knew the movie well. And that was fine with me, at least in the beginning.

What a "trip" this hot babe was—great-looking, slim hot body, tall and sexy, with her long blond hair highlights flowing down the back of her naked neck. She was hot. Toufutie! Actually, she was a little too hot for me, for her ways of living shook me later!

Where we met, I'm not sure, but I'm sure it was at some meat bar that was the rage when they first opened. These bars came and went in cycles. Happy-hour food buffets, tropical themes and everyone eyeing everyone for the dance floor and then giving out phone numbers. Always the same questions though: "What do you do?" There were half a dozen of these meat bars with some enigmatic theme and free food to get people there after their workday. And there was no question why anyone went there. It was like some magnet to meet, giving out your stories and numbers. It certainly wasn't for the free food, yet that was the draw!

When Toufutie's number came out of the drawer, I had a big smile as I called her. She said yes to my proposed plans, and we both had some cravings and thoughts since we had the go-ahead. A country drive with drinks and all the shit I could placate her with for unabashed sex was the plan.

Toufutie has the nicest little tits—lovely, small and perky, with hardened pointed nipples and a little aura encircling each one evenly. Her waistline was as little as one of those southern belles in the old civil war movies, so small it almost looked unnatural but still amazingly beautiful and especially pleasing when naked!

I was getting to know so much about her life in such a short time, unlike Jeannie's life that I know so little about, that it was getting more interesting every time we talked on the phone.

There were so many people that we knew who overlapped our own circles of associates and friends. There was something I couldn't quite put my hands on about all these things we were sharing in conversation, including our advancing topic of horniness. After all, this was what I wanted, so if we can keep this pace, who cared who we both knew? So far, most of this had been discussed at some bar that night and later on the phone. I didn't want to have sex with her associates, just Toufutie at the moment. I called her this morning confirming that I'd pick her up in an hour for a drive to the country. It was the start of the weekend and just a few cars on the road as I drove to her place.

"You found me!" Toufutie said, standing on the doorway of her apartment.

"Yes, it wasn't hard. We're pretty close. Nice shorts," I said.

I had to say something, for her legs were smooth as silk, sticking out of her tight-fitting short shorts. Her body parts were well defined that's for sure. As I walked into her apartment, it felt obvious that I was staring at her features.

The apartment was very feminine in decorations and had a fresh flower scent. Everything was tidy and in a defined spot. Everything was organized with little decorations on different things. I gave her a hug, and we kissed in the kitchen.

"Let's take this wine," she said, pointing a bottle on the counter.

"Good, I have champagne in the car too, actually two on ice."

"Very good . . . I'm looking for some serious fun."

She put her hands around my head and gave me a wet French kiss. You could taste wine on her tongue, so I knew we were going to have more than fun.

"Lets go before Tim calls," she said.

"Tim, the banker?"

"He's my fiancé, sort of."

"Shit. Yes, lets go before he stops over looking for you."

I don't recall actually meeting Tim, but everybody knew him. He had several big business contracts, investments of some sort. He had a lot of money; I knew that much.

We were outside at the car when Tiffany half-teased with, "Aren't you going to open my door?" I almost felt that she was seriously making a point about chivalry and the like.

"Why, yes, darling, may I please?"

"Please."

No matter what her playfully placed request for chivalry was, I was onto this. So I set down her little travel goodies in the back of the convertible and gave her a kiss.

"There you are, my darling, may I do more?"

"Later," she said.

She was smiling like a kid with candy. It was all good in my mind and getting better. I got in the car, put her hand bag in the back, and leaned over and French-kissed her again. She wanted more, but I put the keys in the ignition. I didn't want a chance meeting with her sort-of-fiancé Tim.

"What does the doll-baby want to hear?" I said.

"Do you have Tony?"

"Somewhere in here . . . Let's just start with the Doobies and you can find it on the way."

"Which Doobies?" she asked.

"Taken It to the Streets"—okay with you?"

She nodded yes, and away we went. I could only imagine hearing her phone ring, or worse yet, a confrontation with a jealous lover catching us in the driveway. We hit the thruway as fast as I could get on it, for all roads lead to the country: my country I like to call sanctuary, and this was going to be a "Faulknerian" drive. I could almost imagine living out in the hills near the farm people we were about to see on these backroads, just with a shit-load more money, and then meeting "Joe Christmas" in Faulkner's novel "Light In August."

When we hit the highway, she poured a full glass of champagne. We were using little beer glasses, like the kind you'd find in some steel mill shot-and-beer bar. I had brought them because I could easily hold them between my legs when driving. I liked the thought of Tiff holding one between her legs too.

Off the thruway, we reached a ridge top deep on the backroads with no homes in sight and a level dirt trail with tractor tracks. I spotted it instantly going by and stopped, threw the car into reverse and entered this secluded forest-like drive. There were grazing pastures to my right and some vegetable fields to the left, all looking down to the valley below.

It looked perfect, like something in a Cary Grant movie shot in Europe. It was the perfect spot for a country picnic, overlooking the surfs below. It was an unknown and untamed territory to us both but so bucolic. A Grant movie was all I could compare it to. Isn't that why we were here anyway? I couldn't remember what road I came off of to find this gem, but I'll be back to this spot again!

There would be no people here, other than the farmer crossing his land. This was the best spot on the hill. I set the blanket down and thought of loosening Tiffany's shorts, eventually taking them off altogether. I couldn't give a shit who lived below, for we wouldn't be encountering anyone until we were done with "our plan" and on the way back. We were now into the second bottle of champagne with her bottle of white on ice.

Parked on the pasture-grass, I got the rest of our supplies out of the car: her bag of goodies and a hidden, extra bottle of wine in the trunk. She put that on ice too. It could be a resort picnic if we had servants!

And as pompous as all of this has been since we started, it was simply our "happy hour."

We needed nothing more than the sex, but I was still cautious for pushing this. I was not sure why, for she was drinking a lot—at least keeping pace with me, but I knew my sexually expressive side was going to emerge very soon.

I decided to push it though, for we were into major consumption of alcohol now. And we men of men know that a woman who's given tongue on the first kiss, on the first date, multiple times the first time alone—well, I wasn't going to continue being prudent!

"It's sunny up here! And so warm," she said.

"Yes, I love the sun on days like this."

"Pour me more champagne."

"Certainly, darling, we still have more. Shall I kiss you again?"

Yes, and just take me to bed."

"Of course, let's just enjoy a little more countryside, and we'll get right home."

"At least tease me a little now," she said.

She reached over and firmly grabbed my penis in planned aggression. It was hard as hell, and she knew it before me. I would have tried not to show what was showing so easily, but it was there, and now she was squeezing her hand around it. I was so happy that she made the first moves, for that rarely happens.

"Very hard, I like that."

"Me too."

We started kissing with tongues, lying on the blanket, squeezing and reaching at each other. I couldn't taste her wine anymore, and all I knew was that my next move on her wasn't going to be all the way on this blanket. We did get our hands inside each other's pants, and I was amazed how hot and wet she was. It's not as if we were having sex yet—that was obvious, but the foreplay was expansively wild.

After fingering her, my fingers were as wet as any wetness I ever felt—no smell, just slippery wetness as she watched me put my fingers in my mouth. She went down on me for the longest time too. Boy, was this going all the way today! There's no way it couldn't. I just had to think of self-control to get us home to my bed, for it could happen right here, right now!

We toyed further, tasting everything and moving about each other's bodies. She was naked on the blanket and wanted me to put my finger in her ass. What could I say? I loved that too, along with her slim waistline and small, hard, nippled tits. Shit, this is good enough for right now, knowing we're going to have it all again later.

Getting straight to bed with her great tits, body and the big okay without further delay was in order. What more could a single man ask for? We packed the car and headed for the sheets.

We did everything imaginable, several times. It was like neither of us had been fucked for years. A better description is to simply say that it was pure, unabashed nymphomania, as strongly desired as Jeannie's. I was in heaven, or hell, and not feeling guilty for anything, for she wanted everything too.

When she left my house that evening, somehow I knew it was over, for she implied something about detailing our time together to her fiancé. He was certain to know about this, for she said she was going to tell him! She didn't show one moment's remorse for our sexual escapades, but because her fiancé would return, there was no room for me on her schedule. I was used and didn't even know it. She had this whole thing planned from the first time we met to use against him! Obviously, he had cheated on her, and she was going to cheat on him.

Damn, I never felt so violated by a woman who played her cards so well. I held the sucker-betting hand in a game as she lost on purpose, setting up her next trump play in a game I wouldn't even be invited to!

Ah, the changing of the guard: screwing me to send a message to her fiancé. She was engaged to be married and was using me to prove a shit-load of points. One, just to do it for something different, which is cool with me; two, to cheat like her soon-to-be husband had; and three, to make him get off of the pot to move forward with their plans. And I found out sooner than later for she put the word about her conquest on the street to several of her friends and then directly told him when he asked her. Holy hell, fire, and shit, did this travel fast! Not to get ahead of myself here, but it was coming back to me from the names in the drawer too (who I dated later and from overlapping friends). Damn, I was used like a pedigreed dog performing sex in a controlled breeding cage and then discussed as a conquest with peers on my performance. Apparently, I had a high rating.

All I could really do was to think who in the hell names their daughter Tiffany anyway? Well, my shoe was on the other foot or up my ass anyway. I was used to make another man jealous!

Not that my male friends weren't jealous anyway of my conquistador treasures, but they are simply wanting such a wide variety of delicious pleasures unattainable to them. But I was fucked by someone's trophy wife-to-be and I wasn't in charge! Damn, I was used for my meat, not for my mind. I was meat hanging on the rack that she hand picked.

Well, if there's one grace out of this Tiffany thing, she must have chosen her conquest of me in her mind well before the sex, for she needed someone like me to have it hit home. And this conquest (of ours) was everywhere to hear, even from my business associates. She did her job well and everyone knew it.

What a user we all can be, but isn't that the point? To use sex wildly at least once before dying or be able to do it before it is considered cheating? This game hit very close to the vest though, to say the least. Most other half's wouldn't let this go without major consequences, but in her case, she was doing what was done to her. What a fucking way to go—to force your marriage off with a bang, literally.

In fact, I liked it enough that I called her again, but our phone sex just isn't the same. It was good, for being so close in memory of having it in the flesh and still vivid for our sexual masturbations, but physically, it never happened again. I did love the calls though. Emancipation, that's what I got. The cards played out the same way: Tiffany's use of me, even on phone! Yes, I used others for companionship, sex and crew as I commanded my ship too.

Interesting as sex is, with all sorts of women, I found it to be a utopian desire of single manhood. I learned that one from a nurse, not Jeannie, once. I first met her in religious instructions as a teenager, and then we had a torrid love affair when we became adults, where I always came first and her, second. She left me shortly after for a doctor, probably a gyno-shrink. So the honesty comes out. Regardless of who's right or wrong. It's still who's doing who, using whomever for moving forward while still being single.

Yes, I was used as a singularly prized won by Tiffany to award herself the marriage proposal! Go figure, I was caught in my own web of debauchery, doing sex for sex with those who wanted sex for sex! There are so few females that smart, who plan in advance to use us more than we can use them! To those few, I must toast—to so few of them.

I can't complain, for I was using all the cards and notes in my desk drawer. Using them like the *Phantom of the Opera* desiring to have them all, wanting only one in the end—even choosing them for sex with the freakiness of their of smells, tastes and minds. Damn, I do smile when thinking of my one-day event with Tiffany. She's a sexual gem for Tim if he's into some of the stuff we did, I'm sure. But as the Doobies sang "You don't know me in your world . . .," and I never saw that one coming, God as my witness!

I am gong to be more selective in calling the numbers on the cards, organizing them into some priority. That's the least I could do now that I've been exposed as an eligible, sex bachelor. It was public, and way too fast.

This news was traveling to all circles soon. I know how this chic talk works, and it's just a matter of time before they all share a bathroom somewhere, telling their stories, only to be shared again in some other bathroom chat!

All I can say is that men do it too, just not while going to the head.

## "Horsewomen" Demanding Commitment

I thought that only men knew how to create wars or why we were chosen to fight them! Men being dumped to obtain one *already* in the hopper! That really hurt me, being used for sex as a weapon against others. But to hurt others from the start, planning the pain from the beginning, is not a man thing. We'd rather just step outside or walk away for knowing that everyone loses in fighting. Nobody cares, not even the winner. Fight or no fight, the man who leaves has lost only the moment's prize but sleeps well at night.

I love everyone as a person first, mostly. I don't create labels, and I just don't think that all women are for having sex with or that all men are evil minded. Toufutie dropped me to make a point—it was premeditated!

Unfortunately, there is a breed of women almost as cunning in executing their plans as the Tiffany type.

I affectionately refer to those as "horsewomen." There is not a more vicious group as they jump over hurdles and demand your course presence and to be there for their efforts and finals! It's a cultural must-do thing like eating Greek food with the family. Or for Jewish Sunday brunches, it's a must-show with travel to and from.

Jackie, my horsewoman, came from the drawer's numbers, and has all the looks of a single man's desire: black spandex pants that fit like tights, tight ass cheeks and horse-riding legs with polished black riding boots—tight on every curve, showing those muscular legs and all the sides of an athletic body.

Her hair was jet black and glistening down to the middle of her back. It was straight and reflecting a perfect sheen from one of the club's disco-era lights shining from above. She's "got the look" all right! Funny how these horsewomen know how to make a man react from their spontaneous glances as easily as they did. The horsewomen's outfit worn that way, so fresh and exotically expressive, is a no-brainer to look at and even harder to solicit for most men, but I'm in the game and this intrigued me.

We became lovers shortly after our first meeting. We had danced the night we met, exchanged numbers and answered all following phone calls. I was not overlapping her with anyone like I was with Jeannie now.

Her smell of cotton freshness on her tights, the leather of her boots, and her Love perfume would linger on me and make me a very happy camper. Nakedness with her boots on was the best. I can always smell a little leather commanding the scent of our set when we were done. Just thinking of her using her crop that way, sexually, that's something Jeannie didn't have that's for sure.

I could go everywhere sexually with Horsewoman, except for one thing: a blow job—all the way. She said she wasn't ready for that until she was married, yet she was into doing it, just closer to normal with some good and kinky twists, mostly with a riding gear attire. She loved sex with me. Loved it every time. And did we do a few "horse" themes too? I nayed a few times with that crop of hers. This was an animalistic, sexual release, and those boots were my frosting on the cake like a horse loves a cube of sugar.

We went for many of the drives in the country, stopping only at drive-thrus just to get more before we went to bed. She was a real "rider" in the convertible, and stopping for hillbilly bars wasn't her style. We both enjoyed going to bed, naughty or nice. It became more than a constant thing, for she would stay over at least two or three nights a week now.

Sex wasn't a problem ever (not as religiously kinky as Jeannie and me though—sort of like the Spanish Inquisition—but fabulous anyway).

She had only that one hang-up, she would never swallow a man's stuff. She said, "I'm saving that for marriage." What was/is this story? Could I be going here again so soon in her mind? She was pushing for

MARK FRANCIS SCHWAB

the commitment, I could tell. I knew better just for the shortness of our time together so far. But that was her point to be made, a point she would not cross—blow jobs weren't to be had without a ring! There was too much other stuff going on that mentally this wasn't a problem, yet. She just would not swallow before she said "I do." And I was saying "I don't."

After some time, she was pushing to move in and get engaged. She was using her sexual acts as leverage, promising more soon. After I swallowed so much shit from Tiffany's snow-job, I wasn't falling for another contrived plan being landed as a husband. Period. But damn, I loved the smell of leather on her, the bedsheets and me.

I continued going out with no commitments, and she continued to dress so tightly in her riding gear, even when we went out to my private party invites. She didn't know anyone there, so it was a game for her to show off at these gatherings and with all of my blessings too. This was our game.

It made married men drool like dogs watching food prepared in their bowls. Horsewoman was so damn much of a head turner when she walked into a room and sweet-kissed my lips "hello" there or in some crowded bar. Men love to ponder who she was with before they know. The prize was mine! And she damn well knew it too, and was planning her own results, so she thought and thus was executing her best behavior to turn me on in our game roles.

She wore those clothes because she knew what she expressed—one fucking good-looking, sexy lady, knowing everyone watched her with lust in their eyes. Anything from her, even a kiss, for most of these dreamers, would be enough, even if just once in their silly married lives, lusting for a beauty like this on their arms. Where's Jimmy Carter for their repentance?

The way this was going, much less remembering Tif's tricks, why interrupt a good thing? I wasn't married. My thoughts of having a family weren't there either. I was simply single. "As single *as* single *gets*" and as silly as that sounds, that's really my point about this whole dating scene. Before, sullenly, I just forgot how many fish there are in the sea, and if you're at least three quarters intelligent and can speak the King's English, you take the day for what it truly is, daily life!

Jackie was smart and beautiful, and my lakeside friends loved to look and converse with her. They enjoyed her, almost as much as I did. I'm sure many of the boys would feel like a Greyhound Bus hit them if they ever got down those pants!—especially if she left her booties on during sex. Leather all the way, baby—all that good-smelling stuff and her pants next to the bed. There's nothing like polished leather boots wrapped around you, rubbing tightly up and down on your body. That's why she's the *Horsewoman*. Ride me high, long and put me away wet. And we did that a lot. But I wouldn't let her move in, not in definitive words but more of hesitation for the commitment she wanted and needed to challenge herself, and let our romance run its course. Keep those heals down, baby, heal.

Our relationship began changing, and with some serious thought, so I had to move her back into the drawer for her bridle was starting to feel like a Tom Thumb bit in my mouth as she demanded her direction. I couldn't help changing this scene, for I had become too close—too close to marriage with her, at least in her mind.

I'm damn lucky to be old enough to think clearly and not jump like that just for a committed conquest, just so she can show off her conquest—title and trophy. That's one hurdle I cannot do with Horsewoman. I was feeling hemmed in, and things were starting "to be every minute of every day." As if it wasn't enough being single this long again, I wasn't even through the numbers in the pile! No way, baby. It is the right of a man to expose himself to everything, doing and having everything as single before having to say "I do" in the eyes of God and New York State.

I did enjoy where we placed the course's jumps though.

# CHAPTER FIVE

# *Ages in Time*

WHERE IS THE love, in life, marriage, sharing togetherness, or being just happy as a couple again? And where is all this leaving me, other than with incredible sex with great women not to marry and just another number in the drawer? Isn't real love supposed to be at the end of this spectrum, having someone to share all time with *the thought* after all? These tryouts for self satisfaction and gratification have to lead somewhere, just not with the ones tied so far. Or are they going to wear me out, and I'll become a homebody, bored again in the wrong relationship? Where was my Lizzy?

I'm having enough of a good time, searching though, and this is not over by any means. But it is a trying thing to keep moving on, not finding someone that is the one. Yet I know the treasure is there for the finding. Not every treasure measures up equally for sure. Sometimes, it's just the find that makes the search worthwhile and closer to the brass ring, so you keep looking, reaching.

And there's Lizzy, oh, so sweet Lizzy. My favorite and wished-for chosen one from the beginning!—good-looking, smart, cultured and wanting to be wanted too.

No woman is chosen from sight alone, unless you really can see her soul through her eyes like when Lizzy and I first met. The depth of one's heart and emotions always comes through the eyes.

A true happiness with your mate, at least once you've chosen to be a mate, is just as important as the flavor of the sex you share. Your minds cross and compliment each other. You wait and want the next meeting of the minds, for you crave it together. Without sexual harmony though, you only create waiting disaster down the road. I can tell you from these past breakups that disaster can be worse than moving on!

Your lover becomes a saint in your heart. One that ends the void for filling that drive for monogamy, and all of the truth that comes forward for both, together, and you must share that feeling for a truly lasting marriage.

All the sex in the world won't give you that finality: the emotional foundry of loving so fully that time only builds your shared past, future and present. Once that is in your heart, there's no turning back to being single, ever. You have "a partner" for those country explorations. The games stop, and the reality intensifies in magnitude. The roads become more familiar as you travel together, loving, trusting, remembering *and* planning harmoniously.

This isn't to say that my "singular trips" were not well orchestrated; in fact, they became more routine with new women, for most haven't been down this road with or without me.

I so knew when things would loosen up by the miles we traveled and the road markers I'd point out to them. Knowing the roads so well, you looked for them with pit stops necessary as comfort stations, hidden pullovers as time-out stops, and libation stations. The out-of-nowhere bars Jeannie and I had found added to the fun, just for the local culture and excitement. You simply loved every journey with a woman as your co-pilot.

Lizzy finally returned my calls and left a message—finally. Having no answers to my prior calls, I felt, after four weeks or so, that I had hers on the backside of my pack of numbers. I had several more to go and several already in the crosshairs. But I always considered her special, having all of the characteristics a hunting man would want. She was taller than the others, had a strong shapely figure, had dark-brown hair styled to her shoulders and, of course, had nicely sized breasts, the kind I liked—almost the total package!

The phone rang, and the moment of truth was upon me. I almost was at a loss for words when I heard her voice again from our one-time encounter at "no names" bar; that initial meeting was so very different like the way her voice sounded on the other end of the line. I could only remember her smile and our so fluent, intelligent conversation.

"Jonathon?"

"Yes, this is Jonathon. Who am I speaking with, please?" I said teasingly.

"Elizabeth! Do you remember me?"

"Of course," I said.

Names are names and faces are faces, but this was a voice too. I was at my desk and pulled out all the notes and numbers so I could quickly find hers in the drawer. There were now so many overlapping, it could be death to be wrong, at least with this call.

"I'm returning your call—Elizabeth! We met several months ago," she quickly said.

Shit, this was the imaginary prize package for physical beauty, eyes, dress and knowledge. She was a million bucks of love in my eyes. I found the napkin and saw her handwriting.

"It's me, and I so do remember you. I do, Lizzy . . . on the rail . . . We had a great talk. Yes, Elizabeth." I was grabbing at straws just to say something.

"You seemed like a nice guy, and I got your message."

"Good for leaving messages—that was months ago! I'm happy you called back. I would hate for you to be the woman not known, now that we've met."

And there she was—the very one I liked the looks of best—smart and sexy! We chatted almost endlessly during her call. It must have lasted well over an hour. She and the "French turtle" she was dating were having serious problems. It seems that he took her for granted all the time. This was so good. I'd have to get the date though, for I wasn't about to drop my existing beauties on this one phone call.

Everything is just "looking" until proven; that's my answer to that. This was good, and my immediate strategy was beginning to formulate. I also had to think about simple foreplay I would start on our fist date. Good foreplay on the first date always leads to more. And this wasn't going to be anything like the Tif or Jeannie affairs.

"Would you like to go for a country drive Sunday," I asked.

"Sure."

Here we go again, a yes! Having played the field so well, I could hardly hold back when I said "I'll pick you up at eleven!"

"You even don't know where I live."

"So tell me. I'll be there on the nose."

"I'll see you soon then," she said.

She gave the directions, and that was that. We had a few more sentences of small talk and recaps, but I felt it best to get off the phone and let my karma handle it this weekend. I love these rides, for there's always so much to see to keep a conversation flowing. I'll have to plan for extra special goodies for this drive.

A "pony pack" of beer, for you can finish them quickly if you have to, two bottles of wine, a bottle of champagne, cheese, French bread and fruits would cover all bases. And as always, a soft blanket for when we stop on some ridge top.

I hoped that love would be there too! I haven't even met this girl more than once, but when you feel something you react differently somehow. You just feel *that* connection with the whole emotion. I can't explain. It comes in like a strong wind or burning fire reaching its maximum heat. It just feels right somehow, wanting to break all the molds to replace past women with one—the one. Being two, together, would be better.

I was imagining driving down our road of mutual enjoyment, a drinking dive of country utopia and kissing on every straightaway.

I had so forgotten the pleasurable singularity for having just one woman. These erotic pleasures I have been enjoying, the foreplay, partying and endless debauchery could possibly be coming to an end soon, for Liz feels like "*The Real Thing.*" Thanks Henry James!

# CHAPTER SIX

# *The Third Round*

I PULLED UP to Lizzy's apartment in a luxury neighborhood in the suburban town where we both lived. It's safe for her living here, and the place was classy and showed she was able to do for herself. Could it be as easy and comfortable as our first meeting? She met me at the door.

"Hi, are we ready?" I said, stepping through the door.

You could tell she assumed the car was fully packed and our trip was planned. I was hoping everything was going to be the same, schedules and thoughts too.

"Almost, come in."

I liked the apartment. The furniture was somewhat contemporary and relatively new. Clean to say the least—the whole place was spotless! I'm quite anal when I need to be clean too, but this was spectacularly fragrant, organized and expertly decorated.

"Help yourself," she said walking upstairs.

I went into the kitchen looking for glasses to fill with something. Looking around the kitchen and into the refrigerator, I just didn't get it. What is this chick thinking, as beautiful and smart as she is, she had nothing in the refrigerator and no spices or pasta jars on the counter.

The fridge was near empty except for one beer, an open bottle of water and a near-empty jar of mayonnaise, nothing else! The kitchen was as sterile as a Home Depot display. I poured the beer into a glass I found in the cupboard above the sink.

"I'm coming—down."

"Cool, I'm ready . . . having a quick beer. Want some?"

"I'll wait," she said as I heard her descending the carpeted-stairway in a light, half-skipping and playful gait.

I looked at her and thought how beautiful she is but so lacking of food in the kitchen to offer anyone, even herself. The fridge is always a statement. You can't get around it, for it says who you are by what you eat. And I like having good food without looking further than my fridge. It surprised me tremendously, for I wanted all of this to happen for real. I was so glad I had the cheese, fruit and bread, not to mention pony packs and other libations.

"Well, what do you think? she said.

I wasn't sure on what exactly she meant by that, for this new thought of mine was of considerable importance—no food in the house. She looked great.

"So you're ready? I have all supplies for our drive."

"Good. That's good."

"I'm a man prepared for fun."

"That's even better."

"Thanks, and wait till you see . . . everything planned to a tee. The car's ready."

"I'll get my things."

"Then we're off . . . for any and everything."

"Cute car!" she said walking out the door.

And off we went, down the freeway, exiting twenty or thirty miles to my backroads leading to the country farms, horses and cows roaming in pastures. There's always something majestic about rural life and all their pastured animals and crops. They have no idea how much us city folk envy every bit of their simple life, and to occupy the land with hired help. Some of my friends only see their poverty, but some of us think they have a relatively respectful life with clean air, living on the land they own and bringing up their families. I always loved the smell of their pit-fires burning cleared wood to expand their fields and pastures.

"Reach in the backseat and grab me a pony."

"Ok, I'm having one too," Liz said, reaching back into the iced cooler.

Life is always somehow enhanced with the libation as you drive past such placid pastures and rising hills, thinking of distant possibilities of having a country home, walking fence lines and through old beamed barns with countless antique things left in them.

"This is really cool," she said.

"My favorite thing to do."

She knew I knew that, and that's why we're here doing this on our first date.

"It makes it all seem worthwhile. This is what we all should have to save ourselves from the city one day," I said.

"I'm really liking doing this with you. Not many men know how to look at life that way. Seeing things so ordinary and enjoying them as extraordinary. My old boyfriend wouldn't bring one of his cars down *these* roads just because of the dust and loose stones."

"His loss darling."

May I see things this clear for the rest of my life, feeling that the one I'm with now is the one I always want to be with. And damn, that's my point for dating all of those women, to choose one to love, become a family and live with forever. It's what I want, sometimes need, but what I believe makes me stronger: being a sharing loving partner, experiencing all of those so-great emotions and anticipations of holding hands, kissing, sex and simply handling solvable troubles always. *God, may I tack these seas to sail in love forever again!* was all I could ask for.

After all the great loving and sex would come popcorn and cuddling on the couch with winter fires and a movie. Ok, wine, whiskey and roses to share!

Somehow, we just stopped the car and started kissing and light fondling began without a pause. It was everything one can ask for, especially since we both sought for more.

We had the picnic on the ridge I had found that day with Tiffany. Our picnic setup was to perfection, and the kissing was heavy and unstoppable. We didn't want sex there either; we wanted to share only the desired emotions and the kissing. It proved nothing more was needed at this point. We simply felt like it could have happened already, almost. It was our respect for each other.

Back in the suburbs, we said our desires for the next time to share all the moments just had: country drives, the farmland, comparable dreams and good spirits, and we agreed to meet again, very soon. I'm to call her for a night out this week with some of her friends.

This was puppy love at its finest! It felt good to be that close again, and she knew it too!

I knew her boyfriend would no longer be in the picture. Fuck the old boy too. He is clueless, and she knows it. She gave back his Mercedes she sometimes used and kept parked in her garage. I'll just have to stock her Fridge and pantries to help her love her own kitchen and not rely on where *he'd* feed her.

She said she's a good cook of gourmet dishes. She had better pots and pans than me from what I have seen. She just never used them.

Simply, we'll just have to do our parties at home too.

# CHAPTER SEVEN

# *Money and Addiction*

" NEVER GIVE UP," Mother always said, as well as my most remembered one to quote: "He who has cash is king."

She was the wisdom of wealth and wives' tales for surviving life to the end of her age. Many of her fix-it remedies I've even passed along. My favorite was how to get a sliver out before digging was the only way, so you'd think when you were a kid. She'd dampen a piece of bread, bandaging it over the area and, in the morning, it was sucked out as the bread dried! I never questioned her after that. And as an adult now, growing through two or three recessions, I knew that the cash-was-king thing was true too. Mothers! Aren't they just simply wonderful?

I've already established to Lizzy that I'm a writer for a living, meaning that all gloves are off and that's that—that I'm nothing more than a thinking man who loves to understand life's given gifts and write about everything I can get paid for. Loving what you do in life is not work to me, it's a vocation. Those shylocks and judge's gavels should be damned for their definitive conclusions; however, not all judges handle divorce cases to their credit. It's the money that makes them do it—divorce proceedings and presentations, not their love for the profession. All divorce attorneys suck.

I felt Lizzy was so close to heart after that first incredible date that any numbers in my desk drawer not yet called will stay just that way—not called. I will have to continue some structured conversations with the others to keep them available and then let them slip away gently without much break-up pain. And that pain could be mine if Lizzy is playing games like Toufutie.

You can't really tell what is a game or real acts at this stage. But the chase is real and the love and the kisses are real, so one must simply ride the tides, sailing the seas. Let's not forget the riches of her boyfriend, the French turtle, who seems a very distant second at this stage. He is an aging, double-chinned man, but still very rich.

I called her for our date, and I am to get her at 7:00 p.m. on Friday to meet her friends. This was a good thing, to be introduced to the ones she knows best. It progressed beyond just sex and good conversation as the next step. I'm hoping for *shared love* with this one woman.

I called again to reconfirm the day of our date, not to have any cancellations or mistakes.

"Hello," she answered quickly, having clicked off of her current conversation.

It's me, are we still ready . . . at seven?"

"Yes, that's still on," she said as in a definitively hurried voice.

"Great, be there. Bye," I said putting down the phone.

Gaining ground is always acceptable when finding that committed love. It meant something is growing, for there's more time together and a meeting of "her" people. I'm in the game now.

I got her at condo, and we made it to the bar, mostly on the time we scheduled, which was good, but I know that women are never always timely. She still had to finish her makeup.

It was a nice bar, one that I didn't frequent. It's a bit upscale with toned-down post-disco ceiling lighting, and her friends felt comfortable there. It was a relatively new restaurant, and the food was good, so I was told.

"So here's the guy," Lizzy's friend, Kim, said. She was the first to make eye contact and say something to Lizzy as we walked into the bar area.

Kim's husband, Michael, seemed aware of this enough to acknowledge me with his eyes, but that was all he did before he went back to his drink.

"Jonathon," I said, holding my hand out for one of them and then three more shakes. Who was who, with whom? I didn't know. But their faces had smiles on them, and I returned their gesture.

Everyone was looking directly at me mostly every moment, except that distant husband of Lizzy's pack leader, Kim. His attention to anything more, other than why we were here in the first place, was so evident that I could tell he loved the brown color of his drink better.

I rarely trust a man when I can't see his eyes, especially when I meet them and sense there is no desire to meet anyone. It's a function of their reality or disguise, and it always shows.

"Come in here," Kim said pushing room for me at the bar.

Men always like that, for we do it instinctively for our women and friends to order quickly and not stand awkwardly. Kim was in charge.

"Great, I'm glad to meet you guys. I'll have vodka with soda," I said to the bartender.

"Liz?"

"White wine, please."

He had heard her above the ambient, background music and restaurant noise and nodded to me. He gets a tip for attentive service! Obviously, he's been schooled for me being there beforehand. I felt as comfortable as Peter Sellers in the movie *Being There*.

"This is Amanda and Pete—you'll love Pete," Lizzy said.

We exchanged greetings and light questions and answers. As usual, the writer thing, even though it's technical stuff, had Pete's interest. Everything was going as expected, and I liked everyone. But still, Michael was a weird guy for his noticeable silence. Kim was much more outspoken, not only in her conversations but also in her drinking. She was slugging them down like her husband.

Michael ordered another round as I shook the ice on the bottom of my glass.

We were now in the thickness of Lizzy's new bow-to show. New people, new drinks (hopefully a few more for easing some conversational lapses) and new facial expressions looking solely at me, except for the "brown" drinker. He's a case on his own to understand, but at least I can see the eyes of those who see mine.

Then, out of nowhere, Michael said looking straight at me, "I'm voting for him."

This threw me at first, but then I knew it was a vote for me and not the French turtle. And from what I learned later, it had been something that Lizzy discussed with her girlfriends about going forward with a *new* boyfriend. I felt good about being the rabbit running first, but I felt the turtle was still in the game.

"Has writing been good for you?" Pete asked. "I've always wanted to write my life's story, being in the Navy and all," he continued.

"Yes, it's a challenge to keep your readers interested, especially on technical topics."

"Do you play golf?"

"Sure, it's a fun game, but how one does it for eighteen regularly is beyond me. Who has the time?"

"I like it at least three times a week when I can," Pete said.

"If I got clients to interview, then I can make them a captive audience . . . just to verify the facts over a few beers when in the cart. I do like the manicured grounds though. But as Mark Twain always said, golf is a good walk in the woods spoiled, and I more or less agree with Twain when in the woods."

He thought about that for a second or two and smiled. Regardless of golfing differences, I could tell we liked each other already and certainly not for any superficial topics that were being thrown around. We had good eye contact and spoke freely to each other on a shit-load of other things.

I noticed something at the ending of our little party though, for when it came time for paying the bills, Michael, Amanda and I had our own tabs presented separately. I swear that Kim looked at Amanda with thoughts she'd pick up theirs. I let that roll by as we all had a good time, so it made no difference if I picked up the entire tab. Lizzy and I were going home together. The look in her eyes meant more than any bar tab could charge anything for this evening. And that was a good thing to me, and I suppose to the new friends I have just met too. It was an implied yet unanimous vote to dump the French turtle.

Michael picked up the three checks, and we went home for the night.

Lizzy and I made love like Greek Gods with grapes and all, literally. We're past the intro-hurdles and well on the course. Like our first date, our kisses counted for everything we were feeling *that romance* for each other.

"I'm making a fabulous breakfast in the morning," I said as I closed my eyes with her in my arms.

I'll have to get up early to fill her Fridge with groceries somewhere close though. Hell, this is suburbia, and there's some Wilson Farms mini-store around here.

For the next several months, we became so attached that we spent every night together. It did not grow slowly, for we became inseparable. My place became my office totally, and I just about moved into hers. We saw each other every day, and we were digging it, all of it.

But that meet-the-friends night still sticks with me for I feel that Kim and Michael have some type of marital problems. The other two, Pete and Amanda, were not married, just living together as if they were married and money wasn't a problem. Amanda seemed to have that covered. You can see a woman's control over their togetherness of things, almost dominant to say the least. Pete's individuality only came through with Amanda's approval. She must have felt safe somehow by that, and not threatened by my persona and actions with Pete. I was Lizzy's new bow and was accepted by her friends. It was becoming a love that needed no explanations, just more time to arrange our already busy schedules. It was getting serious to say the least.

That's what I thought until one day the French turtle felt so lost without his (past) concubine and started making his moves again. What money this turtle had, so much more than what I have and always will. Nonetheless he wanted her back. And for what reasons other than his loss for not being honest in love, taking only the sex, is all I can guess. He obviously didn't want to be a dick anymore. He had been calling her house when I was out regularly.

This came to a head one night after several months, and I simply couldn't stand another heartache and I said take him now or marry me. I'm sure she and the French turtle met during this time, but it was not my place to question her at this point.

Women never are timely, but they have something that a nuclear clock doesn't have for exactness. Women can execute emotional time like no other human being on the earth when they want to! And after my pursuit to be in love again, I looked way down in my heart and soul to know that this time in love would be forever, if a woman could ever tell time. This is not a chick to miss in my life, for I truly feel that love exists between us and is "the real thing." So I am trusting that her "internal clock" keeps time in some timely manner.

I could've kept the others in my desk drawer active, just to make me happily safe and not alone, but that is not what I want now. Of course, I would propose, correctly, if she dropped the turtle—when she came back to me 100 percent.

It took more than a week from our little showdown, but she said yes! And with a yes from Lizzy, I banned all numbers into the drawer's archives forever. No master records needed. They'll just be memories of the people *to* remember, listed on whatever napkin, bar check or business card strapped in an aging, breakable rubber band. That's why this is so important to me: I've been here before, asking myself this stuff and, more importantly, that one and final question again, "Will you marry me?" It is a finite statement in the eyes of God; and, as well as a disturbingly final thing when the gavel slams ending such!

So we married, forgetting all the boundaries we've feared and with much ado and fanfare. I gained a family that day too. And wow, what a family. Everyone loved everyone. The kids of her siblings are just so adorable, and they were many. Some of them are in elementary school, and some of them were about to go to college. What an age group they are to me, becoming an instant uncle. My heart felt love for them all. I would do anything in my power to help them or just be one of their favorite, best friends as they grew older in front of Lizzy and me.

When you have someone else's children looking up to you as their family, it is utopian in emotions. They trust you and you them . . . with all the love a family can share. There is always something so special when you add such stature and bulk to your heart. A family through marriage is still a family (again). Now that our love is signed, sealed and delivered in the eyes of God, for better or worse, sickness or health and to share all love and any/all pain, I was home. Time will be time, whether or not someone is on time. It's a family in love that made this more than special for me.

Lizzy's sunshine on my shoulder—bless John Denver—who makes me smile every day, and sharing "our" bed is quite a blessing to behold. We started seeing her family almost every day. I asked her what would be the best thing I could do for her, and she simply replied, "I'd like to know my parents again." And that became my mission. She lost most of that closeness in her past life, not being able to share such moments regularly because her past husband hated spending time with them.

MARK FRANCIS SCHWAB

Well, that is not the case here for I simply said done. We became a very close-knit group, traveling, having dinners and watching sports together on any given, early start of the weekend. We even had all the nephews and nieces over as often as possible too.

There is something in a child's eye when they are happy and content, and I loved sitting the young ones on my knee, showing how something works . . . or maybe just simply performing a trick or two. When we moved out of the condo into our new home, almost all holidays were held there.

Her dad and mom couldn't have been happier either. Hell, they had their daughter back, a new son-in-law and a *real* cohesiveness that makes real families count their blessings. Time became timeless, for we were always planning something together. In fact, Mom and Dad became my best friends, other than Lizzy, and Dad and I became good lunch and drinking buddies.

It certainly was a feeling of total bliss, a harmonious and cohesive grouping of loving family and friends. That's what I've been waiting for, leaving behind a sack of rocks in favor of having a family again. I hardly even remember those families gone in my last divorces. They're gone, never to return, not after all the negatives and knife stabbing at the end of the last one. This time it feels so different. For better and worse, sickness and health and till death do us part. I am glad I spoke these words this time.

Kim and Michael came over a lot too, well, maybe not so much Michael, but Kim was always there. She was a bit of a hard ass though, but not yet so annoying to bother me. She was loud and demanded attention all the time.

She would go to the bathroom during our many parties at the house and poof her hair in some stupidly quaffed-rise and then dance around the room expecting comments after she did a few rounds around the group. She questioned everyone and anyone on how she looked.

"What do you think, Madonna?"

I swear I wanted to shoot her a couple of times just to put her out of her imaginary mind. She was not only a pain for attention but a very heavy drinker as well. Almost as much as me but less than her husband, Michael, at least it seemed. Every time I'd make myself a drink, she was ready, almost drooling with attentive eyes glued to you like you should've known when to pour her a fresh one. She always needed it immediately regardless who was waiting to be served.

When Michael would show up to a party, it was because he had to be there, so I felt. He didn't like me, other than saving Lizzy from the French turtle. But fuck him, it was my house and my life too, regardless of what he thought of himself and his dancing "poofed" wife! He was really an ass into mind games; that will always be his way—give him his Whopper. And damn, this man drank more than I could in any sitting. Brown stuff, hard rye liquor on ice, no water. I bet he felt good the next day, and every day, for when he didn't come with Kim, I'd hear the tails of the bottle(s) taken to the curb at his house. He certainly wasn't afraid of Virginia Wolf!

It was good to have Lizzy's dad as my part-time drinking buddy. There's nothing like drinking with a good man, although when Kim's in her rare form, even he couldn't take that "look at me, look at me" stuff. And that poofed-hair dance is one of the worst things to see after the first few times. It's pure spectacle on her part for her pleasure, but why would you ever tell her that she's looking like a real fool? She's a woman and my wife's friend, mine too, but she's a hard ass. I'm sure I'm no cakewalk as versed as I am, but this is my new life, so let her dance.

I'm not sure of Kim and Michael's marriage. There's some conversation starting to surface about their problems. Well, supportive is as supportive should be and I'm there with Lizzy, for better or worse, to understand and care for Kim and Michael.

The good shit about Lizzy and me is that every kiss is like our first. She's the only woman I ever wanted, being in love for every sunrise together. So I can take the "dancing drunk," the weird drunken husband, and anything else, for it's the total package: marriage. And Lizzy is what I said I wanted in front of the eyes of God.

Who am I to complain about people anyway? I've lost not only the last two marriages and families and so many friends that came with them too. They're all gone and are now replaced by new friends. As they say, "Out with the old and in with the new."

At our last party, Kim had her husband from hell there, with his pretentious comments and conversations. Kim started with her typical jumpstart questions.

"Are we having fun yet?"

She hadn't been to the bathroom yet so I whole-heatedly said "yes!"

Michael, in his typical ass-of-oneself was not speaking to anyone but watching and waiting to trounce as he would enter and leave any conversation anyone was enjoying. It didn't make a difference to him if we were talking cooking or politics. He'd have an answer for everything just to disrupt and make a selfish comment criticizing someone.

What I didn't know, and no one did at this point, was that he had an eye for one of our guests! They were very subtle and stealth about it, I didn't know about the thought of it for another month or so when the same players were at the house again. It was hinted to by his wife several times when Michael wasn't there, but who pays attention to "poofed-hair" dancers?

We were having so many parties at our house, most with married guests, that it seemed more like paranoia than an actual fact on Kim's part.

I could make a couple of guesses, but none really computed still. One thing was for sure, Kim's underling need for major attention was evident to any amateur. Since she was Lizzy's best friend, I didn't want to venture down that unknown path yet. Those chicks could talk about it in the bathroom, if you know what I mean. Men never really understood how women can all go into the bathroom together, at the same time. Somehow, we just write that off as their sports TV game. Usually, we men are at a stadium or bar when communicating infidelity topics, with multiple urinal facilities. There was always a reason why we're there in the first place! To take a piss, not to talk privately first!

Our parties always went on well into the nights with Kim (Michael occasionally), neighbors, friends and Amanda and Pete. They were all lavished with food and booze with post-high school helpers hired to serve the food and clean up the china.

"Who's ready for another cocktail?" I asked looking at Kim's near-empty glass.

"I'll take one," Ron said from my left, looking towards Kim.

Ron was one of our semi-regular guests who has a serious flavor for his drinks too. He also thinks that his jokes and off-hand comments are so funny that he starts laughing first. He's a real pain-in-the-ass type of guy but not as bad as Michael. I sometimes thought they should be brothers. One drank rye and the other scotch. Both were brown stuff as far as I was concerned. Lizzy didn't like me drinking whiskey so I rarely did.

"Great . . . the same? Was that gin or vodka?" I thought a little pre-brevity might make him lighten up.

"Scotch—you know that!"

I reached for "his" bottle, relishing that everyone was having fun, especially since someone else stepped in front of Kim's nod, ice shaking in her glass. She knew she'd have to wait her turn, which wasn't instant now and she started fidgeting on her bar stool, knowing full well that my peripheral vision saw her panting when I loaded ice into Ron's glass. I could hear her raised voice to Lizzy for my attention sitting next to her. And as usual, Michael was nowhere near in the room. I was happy making Ronnie's drink for at least he was trying to communicate.

I used to drink scotch in the earlier days of building my writing business, with the editors discussing my pitches for the publications and upcoming editorial needs at late lunches.

I completely forgot Kim's drink, starting a conversation with Ronnie as we walked away from the setup bar on the counter top.

"My favorite is Chaivas," I said.

"Good one but blended. I like Pinch best. Single malts are the best."

"Never really liked singles, just Chaivas."

"You're missing the best then."

I turned slightly left and found Kim making her own drink, now as the bartender, after poofing her hair in the bathroom mirror. It was the power spot she took over as commander of the drinks. She forgot about her surprise jump-outs of the bathroom when she pushed up her hair. She was making her drink as stiff as she could bear to swallow.

I cared less about the power spot. In fact, I was happy to leave the "tour of duty" and mingle. I looked back to Ronnie who was talking about having the best of everything and the single malt flavor.

"Hey, you," a voice called several feet from me.

It was Pete Jenson, Amanda's bow who I liked a lot. He wasn't really in the conversation with the people he was with and was looking for something more of his speed. I felt good about that.

"Yea! My buddy, Pete!" I said.

He left his group and came over to Ronnie-single-malt and me.

It was a very welcome break from having to hear Ronnie's best of everything. I mean, I like the guy, but for Christ's sake, get a new topic. Ronnie always thought he had the newest of something to have and discuss, and of course, he would have one of the first toys available no matter how much it costs.

It would freak me out if I had only Ronnie to talk to. Kimmie is a loud, demanding person but not as boring as Ronnie in the long run of conversations, at least until her booze kicked in and politics came up. There's always only one side for her, and even for me if I have a burr up my ass that day, for we were always on different sides.

"Well, my friend of friends," Pete started. "How are we doing? Nice party."

"Pete, I'm glad to see you. You doing well too, I trust?"

We each gave one of those neckless, loose man-hugs with gripping arms, ending with a pat on the back.

"So what's your drink, Petie? Another beer?"

"Yep."

Ronnie walked away for he knew this conversation would not include his new toys and bragging tales.

Pete only drank beer for as long as I have known him, which wasn't much before I married Lizzy. Pete came with Amanda, and they seemed to get along greatly. He was a genuine man, not from money and prep schooling, but for his great ethic and friendship of mankind taught to him somewhere, for he truly possessed these qualities. I liked spending time talking with him, any time we'd be at some gathering together. I never got Amanda all that well, but conversations were always polite and knowledgeable with her. She had the money, from what I had heard, but she could definitely lose a few pounds though.

"Get a little bored over there?" I said.

"It wasn't very interesting. They all have the same problems, just different points of view."

"Well, such are the few topics this group has to discuss in life." I hung out there.

Ronnie didn't go far because he obviously was listening to Pete and me.

"Hell, how many things can we talk about anyway? We're all bored," Ronnie quipped faster than Pete could process my thought.

I needed to look at the level of the guest's drinks anyway, and if Kim was still bartending, I could gesture for their refills and not be forced back to work. Kimmie was completely capable and likely enjoyed the control for stiffening everyone's drink, at least for the first dozen. And anything to get me out of that, now talking to Pete, was my plan: keep Kimmie in controlled-power for as long as possible.

"I see your guitar is out. You been playing?" Pete commented.

"Nope . . . just like looking at it . . . I haven't been at all."

"Like you're a rockstar or something" Ronnie clamored, still listening.

I had it out to look at. Instruments of quality, whether you play them or not, should always be visible. They are instruments of the mind that carry their beauty and grace in construction, let alone the sounds they create. The "best" ones should always be out for all to look at, just like a Steinway Grand piano highlights any room it sits in. It truly warms the soul and makes man think as they stand in the presence of a great instrument.

"I see Kim still has your bartender spot," Ronnie said to change the topic away from his obvious lack of musical talent. He liked golf like most did at our parties.

"Yes, and let her have it as long as she can. I don't need to go back there right now."

"You're right on that one; she seems in control enough," Pete said.

"Thank god, Pete, and my lucky stars—I don't need to entertain her too."

He laughed and shook his head knowing full well what I meant.

"She's at her best there . . . look at her," Ronnie said.

Pete and I looked briefly at each other and thought the same damn thing about Ronnie—the man who has to have it before anyone else—and we smiled again, looking away not to even be obvious that Ronnie needed that attention too.

Kim was always demanding, but Ronnie shared the same fate: not able to ever seem to have happiness itself, even while being a controlling interest of the party.

"I'm heading over to stoke the fire," I said.

"I'm coming too," Pete could only reply.

We left "command central" for other parts of the party. And what a party we thought.

From all our past parties at my house, no matter who's hired to help, there is always stuff to clean up in the morning, at least major pieces of some crystal or china to put back into safe cabinets, and to see if any was broken. Tomorrow will only be memories of "tour guests" in selective corners, guest bar-tending, fireplace stoking and paying the help.

All I know is that "I've been taken here," and was in love and had money. I always say you can't love anyone until you love yourself first. What would you have to offer if you didn't love yourself first? What would you share? Certainly not a combined love without it.

I couldn't get the smile off of my face, for Lizzy and I felt we had everything; everything to grow and achieve our life together.

# CHAPTER EIGHT

# *Old Hats*

I F LIFE WERE only instant: instant happiness, instant fun, instant money and instant companionship. Just instant everything, all instantly had with no worries, hate or scorn, just instant everything. If only life were only that simple: instant.

Lizzy and I are still so in love that our kisses are as good as sex. We have the friends, jobs and a beautiful house we both believe to be "home." But getting here wasn't instant by any means. The whole thing seems like a surreal game that came true. Somehow we just keep playing, staying happy with all the things we now behold as our own, including new toys, and each with good stuff we brought to this marriage. I was happy to share anything with Lizzy. She loved my books and guitars, my adventurism and a zest to live our lives together. I felt truly honored, for I shared the same feelings for her.

We thank God, for more happiness seemed impossible, and we were smiling all the time. Happiness is everywhere around us—*real utopia*. It's simply total contentment and loving everything harmoniously . . . as one. We became a unity who would help those charities we felt needed our strength.

It was making us so philanthropic that we started to support the Human Society in a big way. We were in love with life. What else can we even think to say no to, especially animals? We volunteered, contributed and helped for common causes we believed could make a difference. We supported new homes for abandoned and abused animals, and that made us happy.

Every article I wrote was now paid in advance and I had a list to finish. My biggest problem was their deadlines. My editors knew me so well over scotch and theory. I simply had a list in waiting that actually was so exciting to have that I couldn't wait to research the topics as I'd break from one to writing another. They were all "industrial" stories, and they can be so boring to so many, but the art of writing anything can be addicting . . . if you can do it professionally. And those industrial magazines can be so technical that it's also a disciplined art for knowledge of their reader's consumption . . . just to be correct. Being less than factual, having fatal technical errors . . . could ruin a career, and that is death, for such sloppiness spreads like the plague.

We we're invited for the weekend by Amanda and Pete at their Canadian house on the lake. The house is fabulous waterfront-stuff. Hanging with Pete would be cool far more than several drinks and stupid conversations led by others with poofed hair! Pete's talk was good talk and very interesting to me. We had a lot of similar fun and sports growing up in common, just not golf. I couldn't get over the fact that he was now playing tennis, for I love tennis and play every time I can find a partner. Her place was an association of estate properties with two clay courts! Clay is very different than hard surfaces because the ball takes your top (or under) spins so dramatically that you can actually stop the ball as it hits clay on the other side of the net! Just put me in heaven when I'm playing on clay. It's an art spinning a ball a few feet from where your player is, and he can't do a damn thing about it. It's clay, and you can mold your shots. The hard courts are pure speed, and with perfectly placed cross-court shots, you need to use the whole court for perfectly hit, masterful placements.

This was a small guest list with all of Amanda's toys out to entertain those coming! Everyone invited knew to watch for Amanda's rules. She'd give them to you as polite matters-of-fact, and if she'd see something she didn't like she'd remind you. It wasn't a hard-core "Don't do that" but hard enough not to ruin the fun altogether.

"Tennis, anyone?" Pete said as I was just getting out of the car when we pulled up.

What a good thing to hear, and from a friend . . . at the start of a weekend party was all I could think.

"Yes, now!" I laughed saying. "I'll get the bags later. My racket is one top—got new balls?" I jokingly asked.

New balls are what you must have on clay courts. Balls just die somehow in their bounces and spinning-crispness so quickly after two or three games, and even sooner when skilled players kill their shots.

I changed immediately in our room before I unpacked. I knew Lizzy would handle that. Pete requested from Amanda two Canadian beers to go. They were popped and on the kitchen counter by the time my shorts and sneakers were on, and nicely chilled. I love Canadian beer.

Pete's and my friendship became solidified that weekend. This was the start of many times at the shores and at Amanda's. We would all go out to the Lake Club sometime tomorrow, but our tennis game was the start of Peter's freedom to play without permission. As Bogart said to Louie in *Casablanca*, "This is a start to beautiful friendship," Pete could be himself with me. Amanda handed Pete our beers, and we went out to the courts.

I'm getting a new car," Pete said on his serve.

"I love the Porsche, damn good-looking cars."

"I'm getting a Buick . . . for business."

"A fucking Buick? Better be top of the line. They do have great accessories, you know."

"I'd take an Audi, but Amanda wants me to get a Buick."

"*Shit . . . she got you getting a Buick?*" I said as the ball sped over my shoulder on the bounce after his serve.

I wasn't going to push who was buying what at this point.

Is this the way the game was going to be played—not keeping my mind on the ball? And he had a good serve, not to mention a fully loaded Buick! A few games went by with lots of running and missed shots.

"Ready for a breather?" Pete asked.

"Hell no, I'm just getting started."

I knew I was running harder than I should and would pay with some pain tomorrow. I loved the game and wouldn't stop short of a heart attack, but I saw Pete breathing heavily and knew he needed the break.

"Let's just stop now. It was a good sweat," I said to make him feel whole as my lead host without his quitting first.

Peter needed to quit for his obvious physical exhaustion. He was tired and out of breath, and I just knew that stopping now would help our continuous games during the weekend with our other guests, who haven't yet arrived.

So this is life with tennis again? It's happy enough and with all smiles, especially playing on clay, having good food and friends for the weekend. I didn't need the challenge of the "game" right now with Pete.

I thought simply that this was the "real thing," thinking about what Henry James's short story was all about: you can pretend to be an aristocrat looking the part, but you cannot pretend looking the part you are, in costume. It simply shows through to the artist's painting. Of course, James' hired aristocrats needed the money for they had fallen on hard times and could never look their part for it was beneath them.

I loved reading James in college and found that his brother, William James, was the first to recognize social behavior as a definitive science: sociology, and also, being the first teacher of psychology at any college in the United States in the late 1800s. What a family that must have been growing up for such famous brothers to have recorded themselves in history, living side by side during the same era! And who's to say that Henry wasn't the first to understand the thinking's of mankind as he broke away from contemporary studies to write his fiction? William was a genius, if not just for the recording of his sample sociological-testings and then giving it a name and scientific definition. Freud was nowhere on this whole concept, using James's theory as he picked psychoanalysis as an individual, formulation of mankind, as totally the singular actions of a singular mind, linked together by common application to one and another. But fuck all that shit—Pete was getting a Buick from Amanda, and he didn't have that kind of money.

We just volleyed this day on clay. Taking that apart was simply not necessary.

This was a couples' gathering and we're just having fun as Amanda's mixed guest list, enjoying life in a way that most cannot imagine. Amanda could, and did buy everything at our outings at the beach. Everything was expensive, and she had it all at our disposal to use, every and anything you ever wanted at the lake. Amanda's kitchen was state of the art too, being a completely refurbished lakeside home.

We came in still sweating from the courts. All the windows were open to the shoreline. It was music to everyone's ears.

MARK FRANCIS SCHWAB

"We're having steaks on the grill . . . you and Pete get that going," Amanda said fixing appetizers.

"We got it under control honey," Pete simply said.

Pete would just add this to his list and do it in his "special order" until everything Amanda gave to do was done. That's my Petie, my friend handling a rich woman as her bow in his order of things to due. And from what I've seen so far, Pete's got a continual list to manage. Amanda paid for everything and left him alone—mostly—at his pace, for she knew he'd do everything. It was her respect for him, not to challenge his choices for the chores he had been given.

Good, I thought; I can light a match or build a bonfire just hanging here outside, wishing for tennis tomorrow on clay courts and being fed with friends looking as the sun set over the lake. We'll be swimming tomorrow when the sun rises and warms the air a bit. Selfishly, I had to relish a bit, for everyone would want to do this forever if they could. Amanda has her system down pat, which was fine with me because Pete would get the task first and I would help him with whatever *he* chose to do.

"I got matches, Pete."

"I'll freshen our drinks," he said with determination to his tasks.

Amanda and Lizzy were setting the table, center piece and tableware, having finished working their tails off together in the kitchen, and it smelled real good. Pete brought out our drinks and I had the grill lit just pre-peak heat, so everything on our part was moot. We relaxed with another cocktail in hand, looking at the lake and distant lights just starting to illuminate on Buffalo's skyline.

We had the steaks to cook to everyone's preference and with whatever Lizzy made as a gourmet topping; it was unsalted butter, cream and mustard with crabmeat. The smell of potato-onion casserole permeated the house. It was expected to be gourmet whenever we cooked for each other, at least we attempted as the menu would call for.

Pete had *found it all* and had nothing to worry about as he lived with Amanda. You could almost feel their relationship as a real emotion of love and respect for each other.

They weren't married, and Pete was starting to fill me in a little during the tennis game and when we first put the steaks on the grill.

Everything was perfect, and Amanda and Lizzy knew they made it that way. Dinner was fabulous and as good as any chef could make in a restaurant. I looked around, reflecting on our table and what we were doing and thought that Pete has it good as a position, as Amanda's partner.

"To you girls . . . and a blessing of this gathering," I said raising my glass of outlandishly expensive Merlot bought for the table wine.

We had several bottles of this stuff for the weekend. Amanda made sure there would be enough for several servings during the weekend.

"Darling, another perfect dinner," Pete toasted to Amanda gesturing his glass to all of us.

Amanda was providing a fabulous sharing of her existence and companionship with Pete, Lizzy and me, and it couldn't be finer in Pete's life and he knew it. The more I saw of them, the more I was learning just how true this was for him.

He had said a lot about his life when we were cooking the stakes.

"I'm married with a couple of children," Pete said flipping a steak.

"With Amanda?"

"No, stupid . . . I'm living with Amanda."

"Where's the wife and kids?"

"At home. I haven't seen them for months."

"Damn, Pete. I really don't know what to say. Do you miss them?" I said referring to the kids.

"It's hard to talk about. She doesn't know where I am. I call and talk to the children now and then."

"Well, your secret is safe with me. I never met them."

Pete obviously has something good here, today, and I enjoy his friendship, happiness and whatever his "Amanda package" is to him. He is happy, and I have him as a friend.

"Well, good thing you have that under some control, I hope!" was all I could say without judgment.

And that's the way of the world: love, friends and life to share in happiness. Pete seemed happy with his partnership with Amanda and we all got along.

But there's a twist to this weekend though. Kim and Michael have been invited for the night before we leave, which is tomorrow! Nobody told me this until today. They're in the third bedroom suite as Amanda maintains a comfortable house, no matter even if the second and third bedrooms must share the same bathroom—in this renovated beach estate.

Amanda seemed to like that the two rooms shared the most personal space, in my mind: the same bathroom used for four guests. I really think she has control, for the sounds of the lake's tide and timing to know personal things that no one shares when going and showering. She had her ways of knowing everything that happened on her properties.

The thought of Kim with poofed hair and Michael with a hangover the next morning did not please me. I can only imagine her angry, controlling attitude in the early morning hours demanding the bathroom first. I'll just have to avoid her before the morning Bloodys, then until her cocktail-hour intoxication, when the devil takes over. I won't even think about Michael and his expected behavior, for he always came to the same negative conversation. What the hell, he never wants to talk to anyone anyway. Those eyes of his, staring elsewhere, says volumes. How those two get along is a question I don't care to have answered. The girls can save that for their bathroom talks. Maybe he'll listen at the door and get some insight about what a distant character he is. Pete didn't care for him either, but tolerated him for Kim was good friends with Liz. Michael just thinks he is king of some shit and we're the surfs, or just simply insignificant people in his life *he* has to deal with in Kim's life, and that he must perform some of the duties of marriage.

It is tomorrow, and we had a cool lake breeze at sunrise. Pete and I had our coffee and we're standing on the shoreline. Michael and Kim had postponed there arrival to the next day.

"I'm hoping to get our fun in before the guests arrive," I told Pete. We were talking on the lawn out of earshot of Amanda and Lizzy.

"He is quite the ass, isn't he? He has never said a nice word or made any jester of kindness that I know of."

"I just don't get either of them. She's a loudmouth and an insecure dick-head, and he's just a stiff-ass as you call him," I said.

"We'll grill dogs and hamburgers for dinner, unless Amanda and Liz are doing something different."

"That's cool with me, I love both. And let's make some fries with vinegar! Clams and corn too. Hell, we're at the beach, and that's easy beach food. A good old fashion clam bake!"

Lizzy and Amanda strolled across the lawn to join us as Pete and I were now standing with our feet in the ebbing shallows of the lake. It was refreshingly cool at first but the breeze made it colder outside of the water.

"Well, boys, what are we doing here? You look so peaceful," Liz commented.

"Yes, what are you boys talking about anyway?" Amanda said as a direction for Pete to answer.

"We're planning dinner—clams, burgers, fries, and salad," Pete said looking at her answering the question.

"Like hell we are. You two are going to town and getting a prime rib, and we need tomatoes and more lettuce . . . and get another couple bottles of wine," Amanda quipped her menu at us both.

I saw why Pete looked so serious as he said burgers and fries. A lot more thoughts were starting to come into my mind about Amanda's behavior, but Lizzy liked her tremendously, and I'm going to let those thoughts pass. I would like fries and vinegar. Maybe a few loaded hotdogs too! I could see now that we're going to have to set the table all over again, get all the damn matching glasses and silverware out.

"That's all right, Pete and I will drive into town, no problems here," I offered in compliance.

I like Pete and this would be just another adventure with a buddy. But they we're not going shopping with us! Give us the list, and you girl stay home, I wanted to say.

Then it hit me like a ton of bricks: Amanda pays for *everything* Pete does as matter of fact, since he came into our lives. Holy shit, no wonder he has always asked me how I liked his new shirts, rackets or jackets he sported. Believe me, they were all fabulous stuff, preppie good-looking clothes with designer labels. The style was timeless because they conformed to a standard everyone had and grew up wearing.

I knew Amanda had a ton of money, but not from where. I think the family was in oil and gas, and they sold it for major bucks, and I mean major bucks. Inheritance stuff passed from generations down.

All of those pieces of the puzzle just came together from remembering everything Pete has said to me from the beginning. The ski boots and equipment last winter, the golf and the great kakis and summer gear and now a new Buick! It's all making sense when you put all of it on the table! Holy-shit, is this a lucky boy! She's his "sugar momma!"

I love Pete as a common man, not some self-righteous prick like Michael, for Michael is truly The Dick. Pete has a genuine air to him—unpretentious and more than polite as a gentleman of worldly upbringing when he speaks. Amanda knew that.

And Pete knows how I feel about tennis and it's intensity as a good sport. It's a "real" workout, not just "a good walk in the woods spoiled" as Mark Twain loved to quote himself on golf. You need real sweat, real cardiac jumping for elongated times to stay fit, not mental anguish and frustration from selective shots that tease your mind. It's the muscles and the blood in the veins, moving quickly for god's sake, and Pete played tennis every time I wanted. I'd play golf with him, but much less than we played tennis together.

Golf could be just fine if it took an hour and a half, not four freaking hours plus the gambling and stories in the stag room afterward. There's an image for golf as an elitist sport: locker rooms first and aft, carts and fore-caddies, the halfway house for a short drink with lunch and "pressing" the bets. Then drinks and final score add-ups in the club house makes this a full workday, consuming a minimum of five to six hours! It just takes too long to do that more than once or twice a month. And with Michael coming tomorrow, Sunday, you know the fucking TV will be on for five hours, watching a given PGA tour. We'll be forced to answer who is another stroke ahead in the chase when someone leaves the room for a piss or refill. It's been the a "Tiger-thing" ever since he showed his first winning round years ago. Jack and Arnold always played to the ending score, but Faldo and Azinger were younger and put them away in the final holes. I walked with Jack, Arnold and Fuzzy several time on tournaments we had tickets for, and you could see that they were losing their stamina to the younger ones as they walked the course. So that's a good walk that Mark Twain once described!

There's a whole crowd who think that women shouldn't play the game. The girls rejected this concept vigorously. I do think it is fun, for the game has some serious physical and mental merits. Walking is the only way for golf to be true exercise.

I'm sure there were no golf carts when Twain was writing, so his frustration was exhaustion and then mental dilemma of the shots. The game's changed a lot since then. I've played in some fundraisers for over six hours. I might as well have played the nine, with full fees, to leave respectfully un-bored and timed to my liking, leaving my dinner ticket for someone's second. It's the carts that keep it from a "good walk spoiled."

At least Pete takes golf the same way I do: let's just play it, and not so damn seriously.

The last two days we've been able to do that too, other than planned menus for Amanda was demanding. That's really it to life, sharing times together. These are relatively new friends in my life. I just didn't know that Peter didn't know Michael and Kim that well either. Amanda, Lizzy and Kim are a long-time trio.

This whole thing was going happily enough, being so in love with Lizzy, she covered every base for me to not take some of these people too seriously.

Pete also felt the same way about Kim as I did, and Michael was simply a moot point to deal with. So we let Michael do his own thing, whatever that was. We just added him as an extension of Kimmy's "poofing hair" dances. We've seen the act many times, and tomorrow, they'll arrive here at the beach.

Well, the sun rose as it does every day, and I smelled the coffee and bacon. The drinks the night before were good, but the morning's bacon smelled wonderful . . . and there was cinnamon in the air too. *Give me maple syrup too*, was all I could think about on the way to the bathroom for the most-needed morning pee. I was betting myself that the girls are making French toast.

I could see that Pete was just finishing dressing through their doorway.

"When do you want to head into town for tonight's dinner," I said to Pete.

"After breakfast and a bloody, then we'll go."

"That's a plan I like. It'll soften me up for our guests later."

When I came down, sure enough there was French toast sizzling in the skillet, a little bottle of cinnamon on the counter and bacon warming in the oven, and we were having maple syrup. I got my coffee and went to the porch to look at the lake. There's just so much happiness looking out over the water in the morning's glistening reflections.

Pete was right behind me with his coffee and stood next to me in silence, looking at the vast blue space. I just love the Canadian side of the lake, looking across to Buffalo's skyline. It is a world away from here, and there's not an important thought until we leave to cross the Peace Bridge.

Later, I asked Pete in the market at the butcher counter when getting the meat for tonight's dinner about Amanda's "gifts," for we men need to know what's happening eventually. It's our right of passage to know the facts about our male companions, much like the women needing their bathroom talk first. Men are just more direct and timely, safe to answer questions not needed to be repeated. We need to know the facts and only the facts for a situation that has come into mutual discussions, and not a moment before.

"She's *giving* you the Buick, free and clear, isn't she?"

Boy, did that draw a look right away. His eyes said it all. They weren't harsh or glaring, but more like "you really know the picture now?" I could see that he knew I understand everything. His life is completely paid for, even his personal pocket expenses.

"Yes, it's a Deuce, and it's loaded like only American cars are. All options and custom leather, right down to the paint job," he said gleaming ear to ear, as if the cat was out of the bag that Amanda paid for his life.

He told me as a friend that he trusted and couldn't keep anything a secret anymore.

"She's gotten me all the things."

"I thought something was up, but I had no idea! You lucky bastard! I sort of figured it out two days ago."

"Don't tell her I told about her paying for the Deuce."

"Not a problem here, but I've got a few more questions to ask, and you can or don't have to tell me everything, although everything is nice to know. But I had the feeling."

My mind was racing to get the next questions formulated with respect for *their sensitive* topics. I could see he was eager to tell me all things as long as we were away from Amanda. I could just sense it, the joy being a "silver-spooned sugar boy." We'd be back at the house before we knew it, and this conversation will not be held there, unless we were at the water's edge alone and the girls were inside puttying around. Amanda's beach house must be a million or so bucks. And in a few hours or less, Kim and Michael would be there, and I sure was going to have a few more Bloodys or something before they arrived, as well as get as much out of Pete before we returned to the house.

"How about those trips?" I said.

"All paid for."

"And the clothes?"

"All paid for."

"And what about your ex-wife, have you filed?"

"She's not *the* ex yet . . . no."

"No shit? Kid's ages?"

"Two . . . he's four, and she's two and a half."

"How's that working?" I said stunned by the quick truthfulness to his answers.

*What other question should I even know answers for*, was all I was thinking. Married still, with young children. How in the hell does this happen, start, end and not be a finished thing when living with another woman full time? His family is alone without a sanctioned spouse in marriage. I decided not to go there, for those "current" answers may lead my mind down other paths, such as the honorability felt on his wife's end, their lost trust and love, and the sheer bribery from Amanda's desire to make such dramatic changes in his life. And simply, I liked Pete a lot without needing more puzzling answers that he'll give me sometime anyway, but not now, for the "guests" were soon to arrive.

*Amanda certainly has his suitcase all lined out and packed*, is all I can think, and I'm not going to discuss this with Lizzy either. Why spoil a nice outing with emotions that belong to other people and their problems? Further information from my questions is not going to happen on this trip! I just didn't need to know.

Back at the house with our prime rib and other supplies to be prepared by the girls, the sound of car wheels on the gravel driveway was increasingly coming up the road. Lizzy heard the car on the gravel too. It was about 4:30 p.m., and Pete, the girls and I had a few "warm-up" cocktails already. They didn't join us when we started the Bloodys but chimed in an hour or so later after listing to our laughter on the porch without them. We were talking about topspin on the clay, the morning sunshine and passing boats.

"You're here," we could hear Lizzy say loudly, walking out the door before the car was near enough to park. Pete and I walked into the house. Just as the driver's door opened, you knew she was alone without Michael. There was no shadow of another passenger through the car window.

Pete and I were looking out the window onto the stone driveway and could see that clearly now. Amanda was fussing with something and didn't even look up until Pete and I walked out of the door to go help with Kim's bags. She now was looking out the window too. And damn me if I didn't see some look in her eyes, not to the affection for an arriving guest, but to what Pete was doing. The thought of total dominance flashed by me as I went to the trunk of the car. These things that don't touch me and Lizzy personally are none of our business, so I thought. We are here as friends sharing good times. It gets interesting though the more I know everyone. I really don't need to know more about them and their personal problems. But where in the hell was Michael, and why did we not know he wasn't coming? Plans are always made to reflect the number of guests.

It seemed like everyone was having more secrets revealed that I could only wonder what's next to hear? But simply, I calmed down about the "who, what, where, and with whom" stuff. This is too nice of a place not to relax, in a gated community and all; everyone has their own stuff they'd have to tell about or admit to. It's the lure of the lake that makes you tell your secrets in confidence, and I grew up here knowing that the truth shall be told sooner or later.

"Hey, everyone!" Kim loudly gestured to us, with one foot out of the car.

Everyone had a few words of greetings back and forth. It was loud enough for Amanda to hear every word with the windows open. She was looking closely to who was saying what to whom, especially looking at Pete and whom he was closest to at any given second. Amanda has Pete on tight leash, but I'm not quite sure how long or restrictive it is yet, and the more I thought about his "buyout," we may never know, even to our closest of friends. You could see the leash was definitely there though, maybe just not by everyone yet.

Kim was wearing some obnoxiously pink thing that must have been "fabulously" expensive. I'm not sure if the outfit was made for tennis, après tennis, jogging or spring skiing, but the clothes were so loud and bright in color coordination; I wondered if this was another of her "shock the public" statements. At least she hasn't poofed her hair yet. And why Michael wasn't in the car, we'll just have to wait her excuses later.

I can look at Lizzy straight in the eye, and she gets me right away, every time, for she doesn't have me on a lease and didn't "dance" around for my attention. I was hers, no ifs and buts about it. And I loved Lizzy's butt.

Where she got these two chicks as her friends and for why they are so close puzzled me, but again, I wasn't going there this weekend. It's funny how answers just appear sometimes without even asking the questions. And how in the hell do you even ask a question like that, if not just straight forward? I could only think how insipidly selfish these two broads can be at times. Amanda wasn't quite as bad as Kim, but she sure had a way for things to be done. Period.

I simply put that memory aside—the one from last night, helping with the dishes, bringing them into the kitchen from the table and, upon her direction, separating the spoons and forks into the right of the sink and stacking the plates on the left. I did that and never returned for their rinsing and placement into the dishwasher. She had Liz and Pete wash them first before going into the dishwasher. Amanda definitely had a "dishwasher" fetish. Breakfast, lunch and every time it was ever used!

When Amanda was out of the kitchen, Pete and I felt free to roam the counters and cabinets, and we took our time making a great batch of Bloody mix with horseradish, celery salt and Buffalo hot sauce so everyone could have one or two with the simple pour of vodka over ice and a quick stir with a spoon.

Just for fun, I thought I'd peek in the dishwasher and, holy shit, the "dirty" glasses, plates and "separated" morning silverware looked like they were on display in a china shop!

"Don't mess them," Pete said, knowing full well what I was thinking: moving things around for fun. And why not? Amanda wouldn't see them till after the damn thing was done and everything was clean.

"Don't do it," Pete said again.

"I was just going to mix the forks with the spoons in the bin."

"Don't . . . she'll get pissed."

"Ok, ok, I'll leave that alone. Let's just start the damn thing and then put them away before she even thinks about it, and I'll be damned if I'm not moving a spoon in with the forks!" And I did.

Pete turned the machine on immediately after I closed the door.

"Scared you, didn't I," I said.

"Let's take our drinks out on the porch."

"Ready. Let's do it."

I was sitting on the porch with my Bloody waiting for the distant sunset, having watched the leash around Pete's neck.

What a sit-load of bags Kim brought. She was just staying overnight, with a little recreational activities lightly planned and dinner. We were all heading back across the bridge to the States tomorrow afternoon. It looked like she was moving in, with the amount of stuff packed in her car. And Michael wasn't even here.

I'm waiting for the several stories and excuses on Michael's absence to come out soon. I wasn't going to ask first—that was one damn thing for sure. The girls can go into the bathroom, lock the door and discuss it, first; besides, Michael was a dick anyway, and now we won't have to have the TV dominated by every freaking sports program, with cable and satellite programming, which Amanda has connected to every TV in the house. I'm sure she had ESPN one through ten, plus on Sunday,

MARK FRANCIS SCHWAB

the regular channels will also have golf on for hours. What a waste of time. I'd rather just play the damn game than sit in a chair watching, fattening my belly with the spoils in every candy and mint dish within reach of the floating remote.

"How beautiful . . . decorated . . . it's so nice here," Kimmie said when she entered the house.

She had never been to Amanda's beachfront property before today. It was time to get another Bloody, for the girls went straight upstairs to unpack Kim's stuff in her room, probably the bathroom first!

Once again, Pete and I stood next to each other and just looked out onto the lake and the distant skyline of another life we would see again tomorrow. We didn't talk about that, but we both looked to the far side and thought to ourselves how peaceful we were on this side of the lake, today.

"Let's play a round of croquet, what do you say?

"Yes! Lets hit the balls around anyway," Pete said with a smile.

After smacking a couple hits across the lawn to the furthest wickets, we had unconsciously started a game within a game, to see who could get closest to the other end of the course with one solid whack. We were laughing about it. Hitting a wooden ball so hard without any game rules. It was more like bocce ball with a mallet.

"Let's pretend the balls are Michael's head on the next shot," I said.

"Good."

Pete now took really good aim and body positioning so he could hit his ball as hard and dead square, wood to wood, as he could. And damn, his shot not only made it across the lawn to the home wicket, but it went straight through!

"Beat that."

"I'm not going to be that lucky!"

"Luck nothing."

Pete was smiling like a pig in shit, and since we were sharing the same shit right now, I got lined up for accuracy too.

I whacked that ball as hard and solid centered as I could, and one thing was for sure, it wasn't going to be short. As Jack Nicholas always said, "Never up, never in." My shot was just wide to the right, but it had the distance. I could see Pete's facial countenance change, for it almost made it through, if not for just being to the right by an ass-hair. We laughed loudly and couldn't stop because the game now had a purpose: Michael's head rolling across the grass.

"What are you two doing?" Amanda called from the porch with Kim and Lizzy by her side.

"What's so funny," Kim questioned.

As if we would tell her that the balls were considered Michael's head!

"What game are you two playing?" Amanda demanded, thinking that we might ruin the mallet somehow by hitting the balls so hard. They must have seen us from the upstairs windows when unpacking Kim's stuff and decided to come down.

"It's called headball," I jokingly said, and then I looked at Pete, and we broke out in laughter again.

"Ready for another Bloody, my buddy?" I said to Pete.

We put the mallets down and joined the girls on the porch, for now the real games were to begin. And I'm sure we're going to get an earful of reasons why Michael didn't join us . . . but Pete and I didn't care because we considered Michael already here and gone. But that game's over, and we've had enough of Michael. He just didn't come for some reason: paperwork at the office—on a Sunday—was all I hoped to hear.

We were now in the living room as a group, and Amanda was serving appetizers. I had a chance to get the remote and had switched on Fox news, and boy, did that drop all conversations.

"Put the golf back on," Amanda demanded of me.

"It's chick golf."

"It's the LPGA."

I switched back and the girls pretended to be watching every stroke for about a hole's worth, and then they started conversing on other topics, as if the golf game wasn't even on. I looked at Pete, and he gave me a slight "no" head shake and a wink.

"Let's volley a little before it gets too dark," Pete said.

"Good idea. You don't mind, do you darling?" I said to Lizzy.

"Go ahead . . . have a good time."

We got up and went out the back door to the courts. All I could think of was how life could be instant like Pete's and my escape from chick-controlled TV at the beach house. And life was instant, having such luxurious quarters to visit during the summers with the courts right outside.

I must admit that the thought and questions of "How much is enough, Gordon? How many yachts can you ski behind?" (from the movie *Wall Street*) started to cross my mind looking at Pete's "toys" everywhere. And these were gifts to him. The boats, unlimited play on clay courts, the beach house, the bikes, the vacations, his new Buick—his stuff was getting bigger and better all the time. I really can't wait to see the new Duce I must admit, for it hasn't arrived yet. Thank god, he didn't brag about everything like Ronnie did at our parties in the city. There wasn't a budget from Amanda for giving Pete anything.

We survived the night of drinking and eating and thank the lord, no "poofed" hair dancing. I guess Kim didn't have the right audience to jump around drunkenly and ask if she looked like Madonna. The setting just wasn't right with this limited group at the beach house. I don't think Amanda would allow the jumping around because one of her designer crystals might fall and break. And when in Amanda's house, you can just sense what not to do, for she can send daggers through you with her eyes if she doesn't want you doing something, like changing golf channels or standing too close to one of her cherished porcelain figurines. I leave all that stuff to Pete for guiding me around those things. I simply was moving around like "Monk" on the TV show. And for some reason, Lizzy is like her backup guardian, not all the time, but I've noticed she is different around Amanda for some reason.

The evening was much more of drunken talking-fest in a chair, not touching anything. I really would like to tell Amanda to take a flying leap sometime, even if it's only into the lake.

Kim said something this evening that was a bit surprising though. In fact, I think everyone was a bit taken back by what she was leading to.

"Michael is never home. He's always somewhere else. I'm a bit lonely."

"That's why you're at my house all the freak'en time," I chimed jokingly.

"Jonathon!" Lizzy scolded me with her eyes. Amanda was adjusting her magazine rack and seemed to care less.

"Go on Kim," Liz continued.

"I'm not sure but I think he has another woman. Could he?" she asked us all.

"What do you want us to do? Follow the fucker around?" I said.

I knew it when I said it. It was the booze . . . just keeping me happy, so I felt like joking a little further. But this time Amanda snapped to attention, as if she thought I could be serious. Pete wasn't saying a damn thing, just holding the remote in his hands. I was hoping he'd change the channel or put on some music, but he didn't want to go there, drawing attention to himself in any manner during this awkward, momentary pause. I felt sorry for my last words, but I had said what I meant!

I got up and walked out of the room, giving Kim a little pat on the back as she sat in serious contemplation. I went out to the porch for the evening's fresh lake air and a bit of freedom. I knew what was going to be discussed next, and damn, I'm at the beach, not in the city. When I get back there, Kim will come over and cry all about it, if not just for the audience. That little problem of hers certainly would explain why Michael's such an ass all the time. I wouldn't doubt he was fucking some chick every day he leaves the house.

I could hear bits of the conversation from the porch, and it was getting deep with particular situations that just might lead one to the "affair" conclusion.

Thank god I loved Lizzy so much, for *that* could never happen between us! I just never thought of having sex with anyone else. Lizzy was my girl, and that's that. She loved me the same way. I'm sure when we're in the city, if not during the ride back, I was going to hear all the details, so I purposely stayed out on the porch. I really hate negatives in my life, let alone possessing someone else's.

Well, "the sun also rises" as so aptly put by Hemingway. Too bad he shot himself, for I really enjoy reading and rereading his stuff.

We all decided it is time to retire for the evening. We'll have another brunch tomorrow, a doubles game to play, maybe a swim and then a leisurely close down of a nice, extended weekend at the beach house. I can only imagine this would be Hemingway's *Snows of Kilimanjaro* for the peace he saw in the distance, as it is for me here, looking across the lake before leaving for the city.

Pete was already up making the coffee and Bloody-mix as Amanda was preparing another feast of French toast, eggs, fried potatoes, sausage and bacon. And let's not forget those gooey and delicious cinnamon buns Amanda ate every morning. The smells permeated the house.

I could see why Amanda had a fat ass that didn't really match the rest of her body—you know, the ass that looks like they're wearing pillows in their pants and nothing else. She should lay off the sweats. There were bowls of little chocolate things everywhere all over the house.

Lizzy and I stayed in bed a little longer to "release ourselves" with some sex before coming down that morning. I love sex in the morning, and hell, you're usually too drunk to finish anything late at night anyway. You have to work together for that . . . it just isn't as much fun forcing it as a drunken nighttime thing.

After brunch and our doubles game, I made Lizzy go for a swim with me. She didn't want to get her hair wet, but she realized that this is what the beach houses are for: playing in the lake. Pete agreed immediately, but there was no visible interest by Amanda, and who the hell cared what Kimmie wanted to do.

The sallow waters were warm and refreshing to the touch, except if you went out deep enough and hit those cold pockets of the lake. I loved that change in depth and cold pockets to shock the system, just not as much as the warm, playful splashing near the shore while throwing Frisbees and little footballs in knee-deep waters.

Our voices and laughter must have excited the other two, for Kimmie came down across the lawn singing and skipping like a pre-Madonna. She wanted to play with the rest of us.

Amanda walked down to the shoreline and watched from one of the chairs decoratively placed at the waters edge. She was eating another sticky bun! I could see the fat growing on her body by the seconds, as her butt oozed over the chair and that looked scary.

I wouldn't "do" her for all the tea in China and certainly not for a Buick! But Pete didn't seem to care, so I wasn't going to share this "fat" thought with Pete or Lizzy. If she brought it up, then it would be ok to give my thoughts to Lizzy. We finished our frolicking and went in to dry-down and change. It was fun to play in the water.

Pete and I now had everybody's packed bags stacked by the cars, waiting for Kimmie to unlock hers. She was getting a head start and leaving first, probably to catch Michael in the act of adultery, was all I was thinking at this point.

"She's got a lot of bags," Pete said.

"Yes, probably so she could change outfits if she got the chance to actually play Madonna."

We laughed again, as we did for most of the weekend.

"I'm ready boys," Kim said

She popped the trunk and we put the bags in and kissed her good-bye. Why in the hell do women pack so much shit?

Shortly, she was driving down the gravel road and you could hear the tire's sound slowly drift away through the woods. It had a peaceful sound to it, as it always does at the end of a weekend at the beach when the guests drive off to the reality of the city.

Pete and I put the rest of the bags in my car, and we then simply stood in silence looking around the property. Amanda had a beautiful place like many of the beach homes on the lake. Then, the "gravel" sound started again signifying a car coming up the driveway this time.

"I'll bet Kim forgot something," Pete said.

"Yea, like her husband," I joked.

"Do you think he's having an affair?"

"How the hell would I know. The guy's never around, and he never talks to me when he is. He's probably just playing golf all day long."

A car rounded the curve from the woods and was coming up to the house. It was one I didn't recognize, but I noticed Pete giving it a great stare. The car stopped, and in it was a woman I had never seen before. Pete's eyes were wide open, and he was turning white as if he was seeing the devil! A real fear came over him, and I heard him whisper under his breath "Oh, shit."

I had no idea what was going on. The car came to a stop thirty feet in front of us, and the woman sat for what seemed like a dozen minutes glaring through the windshield, which was really only a few seconds.

The woman had a horrible, murderous look in her eyes. Pete was completely motionless as he stood next to me. She got out of the car while picking a child up into her arms with a huge jerking motion. There was a slightly older child strapped in the backseat. She walked straight up to Pete.

"So this is where you are. Is this where the Whore lives?" she screamed at Pete. "You bastard, how could you do this? How could you fucking do this to us, you bastard."

"You fucking bastard," she screamed again standing right in front of us.

I stepped back a little and turned looking at the house and saw that Amanda had her face to the window's screen.

Liz's body stood motionless, silhouetted on the screen door before she finally stepped out onto the stoop.

"Fucking bastard. Is that her," she said now crying and screaming in complete horror looking at my wife.

"No, that's my wife," I said.

"Shut the fuck up," she said looking into my eyes then returning her glaring eyes to Pete's.

"You bastard. How can you abandon your daughter and son like this? What kind of pig are you with your whore?"

She then slapped Pete as hard as any woman I've seen could do with a direct hit across his face. It left a red mark immediately.

Liz stepped back into the house, and I just stood there in total shock. Pete said something that made no sense as she continued crying uncontrollably. She slapped him again with the baby still held firmly in her arms.

"You are a piece of shit . . . you bastard!"

And with that she turned, got into the car and sped away.

I could only think about, as we both stood there motionless, was that Amanda's driveway will never sound the same again when a car leaves. I can still see the daughter's tearing eyes as her mother screamed and cried at her dad!

"That's my wife" is all that Pete could say to me.

"I know, I know. Come on, let's go inside."

I put my arm around his shoulder, helping him turn and walk toward the house. His whole face was bright red now, and you couldn't tell what side she had slapped harder for both sides had her white imprint.

We went into the house and we all stayed silent for several minutes. I could only think about having a vodka or standing on the porch overlooking the lake.

"What a bitch she is," Amanda started in angrily, breaking the silence.

And, what the fuck was going on here? This was deep, very deep to say the least, especially for Amanda's last comment. What were the pieces of *this* puzzle? Amanda acted as mad as hell that Pete had been found here, at her lakeside home, in front of her guests.

Again, I wasn't going there, for Amanda saw it only from *her* window, and I was standing three feet away . . . *after I took that one step backwards*. Pete's wife could have been a "bombardier" caring less who she just killed on the ground. The whole thing we all just witnessed broke my heart to know that such a remorseful situation even existed among the friends of this fairly new marriage of mine.

I poured a stiff vodka, took it out to the porch by myself and began staring across the lake with my eyes to the horizon. It hit clearly then: Pete was the one having *the affair and Amanda was a spouse stealer who broke up his marriage.*

Lizzy came out and stood next to me and was dead silent. She stood like a statue—stiff and completely still.

"You knew all this, didn't you?" I said.

I took a huge swallow of my drink and set the glass down half empty, and we left the beach house for Buffalo. As we drove across the Peace Bridge, I silently shook my head for the hidden irony I had just witnessed. You couldn't talk about this to anyone, ever! It's one of those things people should never tell another soul about. It is one of the worst things I've ever seen, and Amanda was the guiltiest of them all.

I wasn't even going to communicate my thoughts to Lizzy, but I will always remember that moment in time. It was a real slap in the face to my personal space of friendships and too close for me for ever seeing that kind of encounter again. Is this why women lock themselves in the bathroom for—to tell these tales so we won't hear about them?

"I just want what lovers own, for the sun's always going to shine above us," I said to Liz. as we passed through the border crossing.

She sat in reflective silence all the way home.

Amanda is a spouse stealer, and Pete's wife and children are the victims from this, and there's no disputing that. Amanda swooped in and bought him, lock, stock and barrel!

# CHAPTER NINE

# *Imaginary Beings*

I CAN'T HELP asking what is it that we're all doing here—the same things: changing chairs to sit in while watching "poofed-hair dancing" by Kim and telling the same stories to the same people, as we think we know them? I'm not complaining, just having a few serious questions about some moral issues between Lizzy's and our friends. I am now questioning some of the things we do together too, for the only thing that seems to be changing is who has more money and what gossip we can't share anymore.

The secrets are not really secret anymore either. It's just how long it took for them to come out and who you can pin down as the *first* one who told it. It's a game not being first. You're okay if you're the *second* to tell, but definitely not the first . . . for if you are first, then you become the object of tidbits and nonsense blame over all rumors. And mostly that's what it is: nonsense, unless there is infidelity involved and families are affected like Pete's, but we never saw or heard from his wife and children again.

There are a few significant stories out there, and Michael has become one of them! His behavior is becoming more discussed within the group, yet denied more and more by him personally. At least he is talking to "his mandated" group more than less now at our parties, for he is showing up more frequently . . . just not at the beach houses, and those gatherings aren't every weekend now.

I am happy to say that tennis is still good for me, for I've joined a league to fill in the gaps from my games with Pete, which are somewhat on hold. He and Amanda still come to our parties in the city, and I am happy for that. Amanda doesn't want any questions or looks from me—looks like the one that I gave her at the beach house which said it all that fatal day, meeting Pete's wife.

But this whole damn question about Michael is the hot topic now among us all. He has eyes on him from everywhere, wondering if anything is true, from all of us. Everyone belongs to some golf club—me for tennis—that we all share our "reciprocal rights" to entertain. Michael's not been seen playing golf on any of these, yet his story is being somewhere on some course for his explanations of his absence to Kim.

I like our clubs for their ambiance, service and no-cash allowed policy, just a signature. You could sign at theirs and have it billed to yours, and you're not being charged for at least a month later. It was our system for delaying the presentation of the bill (which Hemingway expressed distain for in The Sun Also Rises), and that was fine with me, for we were going to someone's club almost weekly.

It was a "cult" thing with us to invite someone who didn't belong to the clubs. Mostly, they were clients of some sort who always wanted to "see" inside this snobby delicacy. We'd mostly always accommodated our friends' requests, if they requested their guests to play with them. In Buffalo and the surrounding area, we had a good dozen or so and one more in Canada that was close enough for a round and lunch and then back across the border before dark. They held The Canadian Open there a few times, and it is one of our clubs on the must-play list. I loved it though, when asked to play tennis instead of golf, for we all had great courts too, many with manicured clays.

If it were true about Michael and his affair, his golf playing could easily be reported to Kim through the men's vast grapevine. I must admit that even I was asking my club members if he was there on the days Kim said he'd play.

Kim was coming over more now than ever, but now openly asking everyone if they saw Michael after she had a few cocktails. The cocktails are how she loosened herself up. And if all was okay with no reports, she'd drink more and become Madonna regardless if there was a party or not. She became a fixture at our house, and unfortunately, I was taking care of two women because Lizzy was absorbing her pain too.

I liked and disliked Kimmie equally, it's just that she's entering our lives and it's a little hard to deal with when she cries all the time. And if it were true about Michael, we'd all have to cry.

I've been there—lost all of the "married family" before, and this wasn't going to be good for anyone or at the country clubs we all belonged to either. And then the division of money, assets and friends would begin. That is one of the worst things to see, other than Pete's payday at the beach, that anyone should ever witness.

Our lives should never have to be divided that way, whether or not someone divorces, at least not to divide the friends we shared together. Everyone's been together for a good long time just to have one asshole fuck up the things we all shared. But that's what happens 51 percent of the time statistically. The words just become "for the worst" instead of "for better or worse."

How could you look at yourself in the mirror if you were cheating like Michael's now suspected? He has "watchers," so he better not be cheating, for time is going to catch him if he has another woman. Time will be his enemy, let alone his wife, who's now constantly drunk and usually at my house.

I love AA and the people who need it, especially if they don't try converting everyone in the eyes of God. Firstly, they can always drive someone home, and secondly, they can be the first to tell you when you're full of shit too! Just don't "temperance" upon me. We take the bad with the good. And both are always there, that's why you marry—to help and care for each other during all of the bad times too.

We found ourselves at the clubs so frequently now that it was getting expense in my mind, but all these boys had money from family and inheritance somewhere. I paid for myself as we went along. Lizzy was out at the clubs almost every day and would come home with some new golf outfits weekly. I'd only buy the clothes there if I forgot to wear something for the game or it was on sale. It was the signing that made it instant and entertaining.

In our male group, I was their real friend—somewhat pretentious for world affairs and innovations in use that nobody knew about yet—a really safe and fun guy to share time with. I wasn't rich from family monies and that didn't bother most of the boys, except Ronnie who always pretended to have it all. At least I was making good friends despite what I saw raising with the Michael thing, for sides were clearly being taken as if he was a man's man in sexual conquest. I didn't need to say what I did before I was married to Elizabeth. Amanda is still on my suspect list even though I know Pete's family was benefiting from her money now.

In the locker rooms, we would cross-check facts first about Michael and what course he was playing today, not being with us. We were all on missions from our wives to be alert before it became their "locked-door bathroom" discussions. That's when real rumors begin and our chicks create their plan of actions—and for what? I'm not sure. From my last two marriages, I can only guess "wasting the fucker," in addition to torturing him first. Women can hate you so much that whether you're alive or dead, torture can still be an option. I'm not going there, ever again. My heart would fail if not my soul.

Pete and Amanda came to our next party. It was a theme party: golfing jokes if I remember it right. It was my birthday, and I got a head-holder balls-connecter toy to play golf better while learning to keep your head down. Pete had given it to me, and we laughed so much later that neither of us ever wanted to remember that day in the driveway.

The "hair-poofer" was in great form, and Michael was talking a lot more and smiling too. He was having a conversation with a small group of women before he came over to the bar.

"John, can I have a rye . . . please."

"Hey, sure. Want ice and a splash?"

"Crushed, no water, please."

"I'll switch for you, not a problem," I said, switching the ice maker to Crushed Ice for his drink only.

"You still writing books . . . or something like that?"

"Magazines . . . industrial stuff."

"I thought it was headline copy."

"That's for newspapers and ads," I said.

He had not a care for who I was or what I did, and this was the one who "voted" for me when I first met them with Lizzy.

"How's golf?" I said, laughing to myself because every course was covered.

"Almost all birdies last week and eagled three times since I started the year."

"Where was that? What about this week?"

I was in the bartender's spot and had control of all the alcohol. And with that statement, the conversation broke to a halt, which was okay with me. In fact, I wanted to circulate and talk with our guests, and I wanted to ask a few "select" people if Michael was at their club this week, for I overheard Kim telling Lizzy earlier this evening that he was gone after lunch and not home till dinner three times.

Crossing the family room while leaving the bar unattended, I stopped at Amanda and Pete, who were staying close-at-hand together.

"And how's the party, guys?"

"Nice one," Pete said.

"It's nice."

"Thank you, Amanda. Did you get a chance to eat the food?"

I had to ask, for Lizzy and I really set this one high on the hog. We had caviar, smoked salmon, spiral honey-basted ham and, of course, those potatoes that we had at our beach brunches. It is Lizzy's recipe.

"I squeezed the eggs out of the fish myself."

"That's disgusting," Amanda replied.

"Then don't eat them, but the caviar is real good, from the Caspian Sea I think. Pete, you want to play tennis at the club this week?"

"Yes, let's do that . . . Is it all right with you?" he said looking at Amanda.

"Go ahead, just make sure you're back for dinner, so don't dally."

"Great, everybody agrees. Let's do Tuesday about noon. We'll do lunch too. Now eat some more food, please."

We all certainly eat and drink well; now, if we all could just behave well. If we just could find someone who has seen Michael during those days out playing golf, we could get that over with too. I'm not expecting to find that answer first, but it sure is nice when you're the second to know. I would only tell Lizzy, me being the second to hear. Since the girls were into the LPGA stuff and played at all the clubs weekly, maybe I should ask Lizzy after everyone's left, for it sure wasn't coming from any of the boys tonight. The girls have their own network that's much better than ours, for they all just *lock that door* together and get it out. Men don't ever lock the doors. How can women say and actually mean "swear you won't tell a soul?" Guy to guy, that's possible; girls to girls and it's over.

I bounced between the few guy groups of conversation, and no one had any knowledge to speak of except that he was playing in one of the Southtown courses last week. That's all I had on Michael this evening, so far. I'm not voting for him because he simply thinks that he's the king wasp—unfortunately, one that someone is going to swat sometime soon.

When Lizzy and I saw the last guest out of the door that evening, we went into the kitchen together to check on how all the mess was stacked and made ready by the help for any hand washing. The crystal was never put in the dishwasher, neither was the china. We always had the help rinse and stack everything on the counter, and then we would clean and put them away together. Sometimes we would have everything washed and dried by the help, but we liked doing it together as something shared to recap our parties.

It's our tender love time for each other, after a good party, and we surrender ourselves to each other in honesty and joyful tasks, cherishing our life and marriage. We often took this time for little kisses and hugs for each other.

"Everything went well, don't you think?" I said.

"Everyone had a fabulous time. I'm so glad Kim and Michael came . . . and Amanda and Pete. They've all been so quiet lately."

"Such is the nature of the beast."

"Did you get a chance to eat?"

"Yes."

I really didn't have enough for doing the duties of the host, making sure everyone had enough for themselves. I was nibbling on just about anything left.

"How did you and Michael get along? I saw you talking."

"Like the usual bullshit he and I say to each other."

"It seemed pleasant."

"About as non-confrontational as pleasant does. Do you know anything yet? You and Kim were talking a lot."

"She is convinced he's having an affair."

"Hear anything new other than golf?"

"He came home one night after nine. He stayed to play cards."

"Sounds like he doesn't want to be around her."

"She's so lonely."

"Thank god we don't have that problem."

We stopped with the dishes for a moment and kissed and hugged each other strongly.

"We need to talk about Amanda. What's the gig here? And Pete too? You know I like Pete," I said.

"About what?"

"Come on honey. You know. She has a shit-load more money than you have let out."

"I didn't say that."

"That's my point. After talking to the club boys, they say she has about 30 million! I could tell by the houses and gifts to Pete, but I didn't know it was that much."

"The grandfather sold his gas company in the Gulf . . . and she inherited it."

"No wonder she golfs in Florida all the time and keeps asking you to go to Lauderdale. Well, next time we'll both go, if Pete's wife doesn't kill him first. And what's the story on that? Did she actually buy Pete?"

"Yes, she was so lonely."

"So let's wreck a marriage."

"They were having problems anyway."

"Who doesn't, other than us? I'd say he didn't have enough, and now he has a new Buick after all the trips to come home to. He certainly has it cushy. But that day at the beach . . . is Amanda just going to buy her off too?"

"Looks like it."

"Darling, that's not right. There's something really wrong with that—stealing someone's spouse just because you're lonely. What about his children? Is that included too? No, don't answer. I'm sure . . . when that kind of money is included. And that doesn't make it right!"

"Don't say anymore," Lizzy said.

"What, that Amanda's a spouse stealer who broke up a family because she was lonely? It seems that I'm not the only one who cares. I'm getting bits and pieces everywhere just talking about Michael. Won't that be a bitch if he was cheating too! That certainly would explain a lot about her Madonna fixation. I'd leave her too."

"Ok, I see your point."

This whole thing was becoming distressing to even think about—the shallowness of it all—for the four of them bothered me greatly. And forget Michael. He's beyond reach. The others are our fiends, and I have to turn a blind eye for now, but what happened to the meaning of marriage and the vows we've all taken? How about just working it out? In Pete's case, the money speaks for itself. He's a victim too, let alone his wife and children—those poor kids having to grow up understanding that daddy left them for simple money. I don't care how much Amanda is giving him so he is taken care of; that's not the point here. It was the money that fucked up their daddy, not family problems. I have never been tempted that way and hope to god never to see such temptations in front of me. Life is happier than just the money. And to buy a spouse just because you're lonely? Give me a break. That is not on the horizon.

I'm not a marriage councilor and never would want that job. I'd rather be an asshole attorney forcing some stupid viewpoint with weak evidence—as if there's really a lot of difference! The case about Michael is still a weak one, even if he does come home late. But on the other hand, the facts about Amanda—or should I say Pete—are clearly on the table and becoming more of a topic to discuss under the table, if not just to reference between Lizzy and me privately.

Needless to say, that is not how I ever want to be viewed: cheating and stealing my way through life. *How lonely could the reality of that be when you wake up one day, looking into the mirror?* Simply, as much money as they have to spend endlessly, I feel sorry for them for what they have done not only to themselves but also to those they are affecting around them. Lizzy and I, now that we have all the bases on the table for mutual love and understanding between us—I'll just let this ride. I certainly don't want this affecting our life any more than our hypothetical last discussions.

"Let's put the rest of this away in the morning, it's after two!"

"I'm tired too," Lizzy said.

We set everything down that was cleaned but not put away and went upstairs for the night. We held hands going up the stairs.

Several weeks went by and Kim was over to the house at least four times a week, crying or dancing, looking like a fat-growing Madonna. She was always drinking heavily. Sometimes she'd do all three in the same evening. The word on the circuit was that Michael was seeing someone, but we could not find out who it was. If someone did know who she was, nobody was telling. They didn't want to be the "first" I'm sure.

I thank the sports gods because my favorite hat can be used for either tennis or golf, and a good hat gives you many comforts.

The beach was becoming a destination again, now that the pressure was over regarding Pete's wife, who simply faded away never to be spoken about again, on Amanda's insistence. The rumors were left for Michael, and if I never heard anything about that one, it wouldn't bother me, and I wished I wouldn't. As close as Kim and Lizzy are, that's an impossibility. I would just nod about it once in a while when it came up in conversation and would try to change the subject or leave the room.

We were having a great summer at the beach this season. Tennis, swimming, croquet, food and booze. Those sticky buns though, I did not eat. The booze I did like. And we definitely hit that hard. Pete and I enjoyed our time away from the girls with cocktails in hand, even if we were just in the other room or on Amanda's porch. Pete still acted completely different when she was standing next to him. He seemed to be happier and freer with his conversation and opinions with just me by his side.

The only time I really wanted to be alone was when lying on the beach tanning, no matter how many people were there. In the water was a different story, for you counted on the people to play a game or save your life. Even Amanda, now, would join the swim partying occasionally. Life was happy again, at least until we'd returned to the city and it's pretentious atmosphere of who was making more money or cheating to improve an endless cycle of unnecessary competition.

We all knew the fall colors would come soon enough as summer advanced. Then the inevitable closing of the houses would begin. But one thing hit us all like a ton of bricks to learn about at the end of this season.

Pete became sick, very sick. He and Amanda kept that real quiet for as long as they could, and Liz and I didn't know until the full story late in the season. I thought he was slowing down on his serves, and he never gained weight, like Amanda has, even from eating all those huge breakfasts that were prepared every morning.

Pete would even ask for extra icing on his sticky buns, and since they were always made from frozen dough, it was kept stocked. In fact, he was as thin as a rail, and either I didn't notice it happening or he lost it in one week! You could see it in his face.

He had Leukemia, but I wasn't told until later. It hurt me greatly because I couldn't do anything about it, not a damn thing to help my friend. Apparently, no one could. His spleen and liver were a mess, I guess. We all just didn't talk about it. We enjoyed him in the increasing stages with his lessening mobility. We sat on the porch and talked a lot about our past games of tennis and who was playing good golf, and the leaders on the PGA circuit. We now spent more time watching sport channels than we did standing on the porch overlooking the lake. He always had cigarettes and his favorite beer next to him—Amanda made sure of that. Pete and I sat in our chairs watching golf on television for the last half of summer that year. He confided in me that he regretted much about leaving his wife and children and had thought about returning home several times but couldn't muster the strength. He also told me that when he brought the topic up to Amanda, that's when she'd take him on even more expensive trips they'd do several times a year. Amanda always convinced him he was better off with her, for the sake of his comfort and growing illness, and he'd agreed.

As he told me, it was a "confessional" of some sort I knew, but I couldn't pass judgment other than to say that at least he thought of his family and had made sure Amanda had provided for some financial stability for the children. I was honest in saying that it didn't make it right in the eyes of God, and he agreed with me in an expressed remorse. We left it at that.

Pete died at the end of fall, and we buried him just as the snow began. The ground was frozen, and I could only think that at least he is in a compact, comfortable and secure place now. I drove our group to and from the ceremonies in his Buick. It was a nice car like Pete was a nice friend—one I will never forget as long as I live. The fact that Amanda broke up his marriage and stole him with her money didn't matter anymore, for I had known him well and he is now gone, buried here in Canada at a nearby lakeside cemetery.

It looked like a long winter ahead, as Buffalo usually has. I decided to retire my favorite tennis hat to help with my sadness and memories of Peter. Somehow, it always made me think badly of Amanda when I wore it. The game of life was changing with the times.

We already have too many problems still on the table. Everyone was moving either forward or in reverse it seemed, remembering my past loves, paying for our clubs and the Michael situation still unresolved. I didn't want this shit to affect my love and life with Lizzy, for Lizzy has become my life—metaphorically speaking. Peter's death took a lot out of all of us. Elizabeth knew that only love for each other was the answer

MARK FRANCIS SCHWAB

to real happiness, not money, and we were holding each other's hand whenever we were out walking together. I kept saying to myself, "God, I will love her for the rest of my life." My love for her has become my religion. I'd rather die than have any hurt ever come her way. Call it silly, but better me then her.

Peter's death had something for everyone, and we all knew it. His friendship, infidelity, companionship and sportsmanship had touched us all. We lived with his life and pain as our friend, and nothing can change that, even as he's gone. Amanda's money, and his family were clearly understood why he took it—but Pete's Duce will always be in my mind, having driven it home from his funeral with a smile for having known him.

# CHAPTER TEN

# *Different Sides*

THERE'S SOMETHING ADRIFT, and it wasn't wood on the lake. Attitudes have hardened, big time. Money was more important than sex it seemed in most of everyone's opinion, at least with the men at the club urinals for asking who has what business information to share. We all seemed to be aging heavily and saying the same damn things with less tolerance, just wanting more and more money. And mine was constant so it was comfortable but not growing. The only increases for me were playing more golf. No one seemed to play tennis anymore.

As far as Michael's affair, it simply was not proven yet. If we were only at the same course he said he was, with similar tee times, we could prove his whereabouts and end this waste of our time that Kim was orchestrating through our girls.

If I thought any more about death and infidelity along with my own deadlines, I'd turn gray like all of my aging friends in front of me. Money is not the answer. And since I've been losing my hair until the invention of Rogaine, I certainly didn't want to become gray too! Gray is from growing old or from very stressful living. I was not gray and just happy enough *not* to be bald!

One thing for sure, we certainly were not going to be anywhere near Amanda's scale of wealth, or weight . . . ever—maybe just a select few of our other friends. I am a writer not the owner of the industry. It didn't bother me in the least for I wasn't chasing anything, certainly not now. I considered Lizzy's and my life perfect the way it is. If anyone wanted to be something else, who am I to stop them? These are our friends though, some to have and some to have not as much. I didn't want to change a thing.

We all were having parties at the clubs and vacations we'd now book together as alternative sites. It just seemed the thing to do since everyone wanted to show off some wealth. Order anything, even off the menu, and they'd make it. It was just that kind of service—bar nothing. The resorts we frequented were usually deep in the mountains with fabulous views for every awaking moment. Bloodys in the morning, wine in the afternoon and mixed drinks and gourmet food in the evening hours were standard fare. Every one of our rooms we're also stocked with goodies. At the end of our stay, we'd finish all that was left in someone's suite before we'd leave. We would alternate rooms as we changed seasons on our vacations.

It was a thing every year for a good while, and then somehow it drifted to every time we could. We talked a lot about the next time we all could get there together, but it became less and less that Lizzy and I were starting to go vacationing alone. And it was expensive, especially when you add all the airfare and cars in, but not too bad, for the services of the resorts were top shelf. That always made the money seem less important for the quality of life Lizzy and I were sharing. We'd just both contribute to make it happen.

There were many excuses from those who stopped going. The one I remember most was "How many dinners and breakfasts can you eat?" What a stupid thought. He could play a multitude of sports from golf and tennis to fly fishing and skeet shooting. Not to mention taking a good walk in the woods!

I always played eighteen holes of golf with a cart, unless it was some course that made you walk with a caddie, and we did a few of those once in a while, but the greens' fees were high as hell. Golf with drinks before, carts, halfway house fill-ups and then more drinks as we added up the scores were almost not worth it. I'm not complaining, just recognizing how seriously some people take the game of golf. To me, the betting part sucked. Golf is improving your score and playing it for yourself, not to be the best and take money from someone who isn't.

Too bad more of our group didn't play tennis. If you want to sweat over something, then that's the game for it, not golf. And try playing tennis while you're drinking! No one has an open drink in some cup holder anywhere on the court. If you are drinking anything, it's water. And nobody bets on each stroke!

The boys were playing golf weekly, and I was playing several times a month now. Lizzy and Amanda were playing several times a week. And we now had to watch the finals of both the PGA and LPGA rounds on television every Sunday to compare our shots to theirs—at least they were. I wasn't a low handicap and didn't give a damn if I shot 102 . . . I play *to* like the game, and drive the golf cart with cup holders.

We had a new semiprivate course open in East Aurora, halfway down to the ski hills in a swank historic community that was all the talk, but no one had played it yet. I had an editor's meeting coming up, and we decided to play the new course Eagle Sticks, designed by one of the notable golfers: Nicholas, Palmer, or Zoeller? I'm not sure, but I had free vouchers. My game was to include a meeting with my editor to cover topics for an upcoming issue. We needed to do it quickly, for they changed placement for a new industrial innovation to the cover story, and I was given the option for all the sub-features too. And this was my breadwinner. I was paid top dollar for these, for they were scrambling to sell this to the industry with short notice for all the manufacturer's ad dollars. The editorial calendar had already been published, and I was their "proven" writer to make whatever the deadlines and stories required to happen.

We did all the pre-golf stuff at the course when we arrived, and we were now in the cart. The place was empty except for a few cars in the lot.

The first fairway looked fabulous, with a left to right downward-sloped fairway bordered on each side with seventy-year-old trees. The grass was immaculate, and the rough looked like our suburban lawns. Mark Twain's description might have changed on this one, but then again, we had a golf cart carrying everything under the sun, including files and libations.

Tom McCarthy, my editor, had his briefcase for god's sake, and my notes were in a steno reporter's notebook, scribbled randomly for thought. I wasn't briefed before this, but we were talking "trenchers" digging big holes for long distances by some new manufacturer of an engine that just wouldn't quit. It had some new titanium shaft that wouldn't break. It was in limited test production but would change the face of burying fiber optic cables and waterlines.

I couldn't get my mind off this new golf course! It was so manicured that you would want to take the dogs for a long walk, if they'd let you. We had a six-pack in the cart's cooler, and I had a vodka and soda in the cup holder. I had them make mine a double, for once I start on beer, I have to piss like a racehorse on every tree at least every few holes. Fortunately, there were no women on the course or in sight!

We both had some great shots in between "editorial comments" to sell advertising in the issue. It was a tight deadline like a few of the fairways we negotiated. The course was empty except for a twosome in front of us, so we decided to take our time on every shot, smashing the ball for distance. McCarthy was better at the whole of the game, but he couldn't outdrive me when I was on. He tried to outdrive me on every hole but couldn't. I had him by forty yards easily when I kept it in the fairway. The rest of the time I would slice into the woods. We were enjoying the solitude of this beautifully designed and out-of-the-way course.

Coming up to the eighteenth par-four tee box, the couple in front of us was just finishing up on the green, and they were very chummy. He'd hold her from behind showing her how to stroke the putter, and the way his arms were around her, you could see that this was not just golf lessons. They kissed little pecks as I would when playing with Lizzy after making a good put.

When they saw us mid fairway, they finally walked off the green, got into their cart and drove straight to the parking lot.

Walking across the eighteenth green, I looked over to them putting their clubs in the trunk and changing their shoes in the parking lot, which normally you'd do in the clubhouse. Then the sky opened in front of my eyes! It was freek'en Michael, and he was not with Kim! They did a little more kissing and got in the car and drove away thinking they were invisible to the few golfers on this new course. McCarthy saw nothing, not that he would know the story anyway. I told him what had just happened in brief and about all the search parties out to prove Kimmie's theory of her husband's affair. And shit, if it wasn't fucking true, *and I had to see it first!* How could I tell anyone first? Being second is so much better when spreading this type of infectious information, and my heart just sank. I couldn't even think about my article, and it's a damn good thing it was at the end of our game for I had the notes now, so I could only think just how I'm going to handle all of this.

We got McCarthy back to his car in the city, and he left happy, knowing that his problems were covered. Not mine though, for mine were just about to begin. I had to tell Lizzy who would tell Kim at the *first* "private bathroom" meeting she could get. I can just see them both now; their eyes would simply have daggers ready to fly. Damn me for being first, for there are no seconds on this one. Everyone will come to me directly, even if they're the tenth to know. I hate this position, but it must be said to Lizzy, and she can take it from there. After all, I'm not in Michael's seat, which is about to get real fucking hot! And even though I don't like him, I'm feeling sorry about his situation for he's about to enter hell.

"How was your game and meeting?" Lizzy asked when I walked in the door.

"Fine . . . I think I'll have a vodka."

"That good, was it? Is the course as nice as they say?"

"Better than you think," I said rolling my eyes over to the liquor cabinet.

She knew right then and there that I had something more to say. "What . . . ?"

"Let me get that drink, and I think you should have one too."

"What?"

"You're not going to like this . . ." I could feel my words hanging in the air.

"Tell me now, come on."

"Let's get you a drink first."

"Ok, just wine."

We had our glasses in hand and a sip before I spoke again.

"Michael was playing golf there too, and the course was pretty much empty."

"So?"

"He wasn't alone." I could see her brow and head twist simultaneously.

"What do you mean?" her voice pitched.

"He wasn't alone. He was with another woman."

"Could be an associate of his."

MARK FRANCIS SCHWAB

"I don't think so, for they were kissing and playing more than golf on the last hole."

"Get out, no way. Are you sure it was him?"

"No, his Santa suit disguised him quite well, and that was his caddie." I smirked a bit but looked her in the eyes, and she knew I wasn't kidding.

"Get out," she could only repeat.

"I'm sorry to be the first to know. You know that . . . nobody else knows and that makes you the second to know. I saw it Liz, and that ain't no caddie he was playing with, and he wasn't wearing winter clothes. He thought no one was there. The course was virtually empty," I said finishing my thought.

"Did he see you?"

"No . . . I wish he did for this would be his problem then, not mine for having seen it firsthand."

"You're kidding? *It is his problem. That cheat!* Kim has held that family together giving him all the 'room' to be a dad—gone like he is. What a shit. Wait till Kim knows."

"Now hold here, this isn't so simple. I'm the *first*, and you can't be saying that . . . to anyone. We have to think about this. I'm not in the middle of this . . . guess I am, but think first, please."

"I can't believe this . . . are you sure?"

"Sure enough that the idiot should have worn a Santa suit to be doing that in public, even if no one was there!"

"I just can't believe this . . ."

"Believe it," was all I could say while pouring another drink, knowing this bombshell was about to explode.

These ramifications are not limited to just us; everyone would know soon, and it would only be true because I was the first to say it's true. And Liz is going to tell Kim directly, meaning I'll have to describe it fifteen or twenty times, increasing in detail to Kim after she's heard it from Liz once. I'd rather be the *last* one in the world to know right now, for that woman will be crying, getting drunker and questioning her husband's infidelity every day in my house. I'll have to describe what she looked like ten dozen times as she slobbers in her drink, and then when she sobers-up. Just the thought of this made me want to start writing my "titanium shaft" article for McCarthy's magazine.

Kim was called and told to come over. Thank god she wasn't home, and Lizzy left a message. This gave me another day of reprieve before the crying and yelling started; and Lizzy, another day to really think about how she was going to say that Michael had another woman and was definitely cheating on her, via me having to fill in the details. I don't like anger or shit-loads of crying, and this one was going to have a lot of both.

I guess the bright side of this was that Kim won't be doing her *poof dances* anytime soon at one of the upcoming parties, if she'd come at all, for this is some serious shit to control in her behavior. It comes with a lot of bags to open and close, and who knew what "planet" those two were going to be on? And for that matter, soon all the country clubs were going to be buzzing. I will be on the front line, bar none for having seen it with my own eyes.

Kim was over at least three times in as many days, asking me the same questions and getting the same answers. Lizzy fed her alcohol, and I made appetizers for her to eat during the crying and screaming about Michael. Kim was telling everyone now, and I felt very uncomfortable about that. I kept playing tennis on the club's league just to stay off the golf course because the stag room seemed to have two sides now: one for "I shouldn't have said anything" and the other for getting the truth out.

Several months passed and Kim and Michael stayed together, at least in the same house, but things were brewing to a boil-over. Lizzy was giving me bits and pieces about their phone conversation because Kim was staying put and hardly came over here during this time. What was brewing is everyone's sorrow—a pending divorce, or maybe not.

I was not giving opinions on that for if they could work it out, they should. That's the way of marriage, compromise and acceptance; however, infidelity is a big compromise to accept. And it is not my place, or Lizzy's, to direct any actions for any conclusions. If only it were that easy to stay detached while working it out together, but for some people that is impossible. I could only think of Pete's family being left alone by his departure for Amanda.

So many people take it upon themselves to make "judgments" for them as if it was their right and power to direct others in family matters they really have no part in; yet they are compelled to take sides and demand their directions be taken as the only possible outcome. That is

MARK FRANCIS SCHWAB

total blindness on their part, both given and accepted, for the pain and problems in marriage are enough alone, and divorce is so much worse and sad. Why people must be first to offer the "right" answer is none of their damn business.

Amanda, of all people, was pushing hard for Kim to divorce Michael, Lizzy was fence-sitting and I simply said it was none of my business and wouldn't comment further, other than to Lizzy to stay out of it. But the stuff between women is an impossibility to stay out of, giving credence and commentary during the group's bathroom talks.

In time, Kim was coaxed into filing for divorce. When she finally served him with papers, Michael moved out to an apartment. That's when the real shit hit the fan. He started to open up as a free man might, talking to his golf cronies openly about it, and Lizzy had found out from more bathroom talk, gathered from our respective male spouse's and by supposed additional sightings other than mine that now verified all rumors about Michael's secret life, and that he may have three girl friends on the side!

All I could think about is what an ass he always was to everyone, definitely to me, at all of the parties when he'd show up. We were always conveniently on the opposite sides of the room rather than the bar.

We never spoke again.

## CHAPTER ELEVEN

# *Trusting Souls*

PUTTING FAITH IN yourself and "In God We Trust" (like on the dollar bill), dismissing the bad signs, trusting your heart, looking forward to the positive and losing all the negatives just to be happy is the answer to life. That and having a love to share is what the world's all about: loving yourself and your partner and living together in a world free to choose your life to live. Your friends are there too, and that's the added benefit—one that cannot be overlooked; and if you are who you say you are, then you can have them too without the worries of rumors like those Michael and Amanda have.

It's those "friends" who get you through things like divorce—and everyone needs them—as much as love itself. And sometimes you find one or two dear friends through marriage(s) that make it to the other side, that being the far side, regardless of hate and war, separation of church and state or a judge's gavel swinging definitive answers, as they will remain true to their friendship. A true friend will always be with you.

We all tried to keep our wits with the times as the summer became winter and onward. Our winter didn't seem as long this year, but we had a lot to keep us busy, choosing and avoiding certain parties for obvious reasons. And in between, most of us skied at one of the nearby resorts, a few were private and those were good times. However, we always made some pilgrimage to Florida for a week or so. When the Buffalo winters would end, we'd forget and forgive the negatives and problems we had faced earlier. This last winter, Amanda was almost invisible.

We were up at the beach early this summer, like always, just with other club members, power boating, sailing, tennis, and Bloodys, and all were in the gated communities. The city life was always left on the other side of the lake. It kept the element of chance to manageable levels, at the very least, respectable, for remembering who was with whom.

Many more separations and divorces split everything into little pieces of a puzzle that didn't fit anymore. Many of us have friends and families who never made it to the lake anymore or we'd see them in the city because of those finite breakups. Divorce is hell, and it should be outlawed. In the eyes of the church it is.

But as I said, this is the beach, and Lizzy and I were at Amanda's half the time, readying the place, sprucing up the yard for her entertainment and upcoming guests. We raked the clay courts and changed the croquet field regularly. I was always taking the rubber boat and its motor in an out of the water, beached in front of the house, ready to use as I did with Pete so many times before.

She always had just a few core regulars to do visits with Liz and me but brought in a few newcomers she gathered somewhere. She didn't really have much going on with the other "beach" folks, except that she had more money than most all of them. They knew it, and she knew it.

Her parties rarely had no more then six to eight people max, with only two to four guests that would spend the weekend. It usually was just Lizzy and me. Of course, there was always the end of the year blowout party she'd hold, but after Pete's passing, it didn't happen anymore.

I was out in the yard picking up downed branches from a bit of a wind the night before when I heard the gravel driveway sounding under the weight of an approaching car. Amanda had mentioned, more directly to Lizzy than me earlier that morning that she was having a friend join us for lunch and the remainder of the weekend.

As the car emerged between the trees, my heart sank and my mouth fell wide open. It was the Buick—Pete's Buick. I felt numb and stood motionless as it pulled to a stop. I had never seen the driver before and had no clue who he was. I heard the screen door open and turned to see Amanda crossing the grassy distance between us. Lizzy was looking out the kitchen window where Amanda would normally perch to spy on the yard for her arriving visitors.

Amanda had made it to the car before the car door could open, as if there was clockwork for this since I was out in the back and not on the beachside of the house. I could sense a form of exerted control by her by the way she looked at me and then back to the man getting out of Pete's Buick. Without saying anything, he kissed her on her outstretched cheek. Amanda expected this kiss. I wasn't saying anything first! I walked closer to Pete's Duce.

"Duke, this is Jonathan," Amanda said.

"Hi, nice to meet you," he said.

I really wanted to ask him about the Buick, but I knew that was all going to come out, and although it was Pete's Buick, cars last longer than most men.

Duke reminded me of a happy-looking walrus just out of the water—smiling and anxious to please everyone. He seemed like a nice enough guy. He had a mustache that carried his smile well, a bit stocky though, but so was Amanda if you wanted to be nice about her weight. I could just see those two tomorrow morning at breakfast over sticky buns!

"Duke!" I said offering a handshake and smile.

"It's really Doug, but I got Duke years ago."

"John, help Duke get his luggage," Amanda said cutting us both short.

"Sure thing, so you've known Amanda long?"

I knew the consequences of that one when it came out of my mouth. Amanda's eyes read volumes, but she didn't say anything to my question for Duke.

"We've met a few years ago and became good friends."

"Hey . . . a tennis racket! Let's play after you get settled and changed!" I said, reaching for his bags in the trunk, eying the racket on the backseat through the rear window.

"Later, just get the bags for now," Amanda jumped in before I could say anything further; and I thought everything said was quite harmless so far.

She wanted Duke in the house, settled and in "group" conversation with Lizzy too. That was evident, and I'm just a guest enjoying life at the beach. I grabbed his bags and walked into the house. His tennis racket was left lying on the backseat.

MARK FRANCIS SCHWAB

"Hello, Duke," Lizzy said as we entered into the house.

Then it hit me, Liz had met him prior to this! What was going on between Amanda's private life and Lizzy and my not being privy to this seemingly inside information? What is Amanda so controlling for? And why is Lizzy not keeping me up to date on this "secret" stuff? I always told her what I knew when I knew it. This isn't rocket science, or maybe Amanda's "secret life" had more to it than meets the eye. I'll have to think about this as soon as I pour myself a vodka.

"Bloodys, Duke?" I said.

He looked at the girls.

"Sure, why not . . . It's a little early, but why not?"

"That's my boy. I'll get the mix going. We're at the lake so who's keeping time anyway?"

"I hear you like tennis a lot," he said.

"Yep, me, me-tennis and me-Bloodys! Of course, me-Lizzy too. I love the sport. Let's volley later. It's great exercise."

"You boys are having lunch first," Liz said.

"Certainly, my darling, maybe you'll join us for a volley?"

"You go ahead," Amanda said to Liz.

"You're both welcome, right Duke?"

"The more the merrier."


I could see that control was in the air, and permission would be granted by Ms. Sticky Buns. I wanted to tell her that she needed to be out there too, but there was no diplomatic way to say it without referring to her almost daily weight gain. I don't know why or who would sleep with her, no matter how much money she had. Summers are for toning the body, not preparing for winter's hibernation!

At her rate of growing from the rear up, it's just a matter of time before she becomes like that commercial by Wendy's Hamburgers years ago, portraying the Russian fashion show. They all looked the same in everything—fat and rounded from head to toe. It was so unsightly last summer when she'd sit in the chair at the shore as we all were swimming and her thighs would roll over the edge of that chair! God, help us all if we got like that!

Amanda, though, was a providing host at the very least, but it was going to show on her for years, even if she started dieting and exercising now.

After lunch, Duke and I went out to the courts alone. At the last minute, Amanda made Lizzy stay to help prep for dinner. Apparently, we were having a couple from the Lake Club over too. I was out of the loop for who's invited to what and when, like meeting Duke in Pete's Buick, so I was content enough being in charge of the drinks, tennis, croquet and the water games I'd simply make up for our parties. My job for Amanda was of my own making, making sure I needed no approvals or additional chores.

"So Dukie, when did you two meet?" I asked him on the courts about Amanda.

"We've known each other on and off for several years now."

"Really."

"Yes, we met golfing on her country club course . . . when I was a guest, and we talked more at lunch. We've seen each other several times, but lately a lot more."

"Let's forget the game and just volley," I said.

It would be easier to continue talking and getting more about this overlap of time he mentioned during Pete's life—and now driving his Buick.

"How'd you come to hook up now?" I asked again like an attorney would question a witness for revealing more this time.

"We've been seeing each other for a year or so."

Now my thoughts were confirmed—Amanda had this going before Pete died, having met him during that relationship. It's like she had backed herself up knowing Pete was a goner.

"So how's the Buick?"

"My car quit back in January, and she let me have it till whenever."

"It's a nice car," I said, knowing that the seat was still warm from Pete's ass driving it until his death.

We had a couple of nice volleys, and I said let's head back to the house. He agreed so we stopped. I wanted to get us back to "group conversation" now. I didn't want to know more from Duke but wanted a lot more from Lizzy. There was obviously more to this story, and I didn't need any more of my questions getting back to Amanda. She'd be sure to question everything we talked about, and I thought it best to leave it there.

An hour or so passed on the porch with cocktails looking at the lake with idle chitchat when we heard another car coming up the driveway.

"That should be the Whinstners," Lizzy said.

MARK FRANCIS SCHWAB

"Shit . . . get out! Why didn't you tell me they were invited? I said smiling.

"We thought we'd surprise you."

"Thanks, my darling love. This is a surprise."

I have known Nicky since being kids and well into my second marriage years ago. The last time I saw him other than passing in one of the regattas was several years ago at the Lake Club, pounding drinks at the bar trying to fix me up. He still is married to his childhood sweetheart, who I knew then too. I wondered briefly about what jokes and old times we would remember together but have not shared in so many years. I was glad they knew Amanda somehow, and I'm sure she invited them as a pleasing gesture to have a mix of people and conversation at her dinner introducing Duke. I'm sure of it.

This was going to be fun and very interesting to say the least: the new Duke, my third wife, my old friends on my exes' side, and Amanda all at the beach at the same time!

I was in the driveway first this time, with everyone behind me coming out into the yard to greet our guests as the car doors opened. It was a Roman welcome—the kind everyone likes to have when they arrive somewhere at another beach house.

I felt that these still are still good times regardless of past mistakes. Today is today, and any remembered negatives, other than joking about them, are history to laugh about. Tonight's party will certainly be remembered, with Duke and all. I'm sure Lizzy's ears will be wide open too. And may I say, *welcome to the party, Duke*! I think Nicky and I invented the Bloody Brunches here at the beach or just carried them on faithfully. It is a tradition we've grown up with.

"Hey guys!" I said loudly to Nick and Sally.

They looked the same as I remembered them, yet they were married with high school and early college aged children now. Love works wonders on people who stay together through all the shit in the early years. It makes character—the kind that relaxes their face from aging for their inner happiness.

It was good to see smiles on the faces of old friends again. I could only imagine what was going to be said at dinner, let alone over cocktails shortly. It all was going to be very interesting.

"Ready for Bloodys?" I said at this late afternoon hour, knowing full well that we were pouring rum or vodka (like so many years ago) before dinner. Sailors love their rum; power-boaters love their vodka and whiskey.

"Look at you!—married and not crying in your drink anymore!" Nick said, smiling ear to ear. "You remember Sally?"

"Sure do. You haven't aged a bit," I said giving them both a hug.

"Meet Elizabeth, my wife."

"Another one?" Nick joked.

"Ok, ok, let's not bring that up!"

We went through the introduction rituals, and then we all started to stroll toward the beach around the side of the house, walking two or three to a group. Everyone was drawn to the lake. Nick and I walked together with Sally and the girls in the lead. Duke was a step behind Amanda.

"You crazy bastard-boy . . . how many is this, three now?"

Sally's eyes were on me waiting for my answer.

"Yep, this makes three . . . or four? God, it's good to see you guys."

"You too," Sally said.

"We're real happy with grown family and all. So who's this Amanda?" Nick asked.

"I thought you knew her! She's getting a little odd," I said softly. "In fact, I didn't even know who was coming till today!"

"Get out. We don't know her at all other than the annual Commander's Dinner."

"No kidding? Amanda's surprise for us all I guess. She acted like she knew you both. Duke is her new bow though. Just met him at lunch."

"Get out . . ." was all Nick could say.

We smiled, not saying another word till we stopped on the end of the grass at the water's edge.

"That's very funny," Sally said overhearing everything.

Amanda and Lizzy went into the house.

"Damn funny . . . she just said she was having friends over when she invited us out of the blue."

"Well, we're all here now, and it is funny," I laughingly said.

"Good to see you man," Nick said putting his hand on my shoulder as we looked out over the lake.

"Damn good to see you guys . . . This should be fun tonight! Cocktails?"

"Damn straight Jonnie-boy. Nothing's changed here," Sally said with a grin.

We walked across the grass and went through the screened porch into the house to get the drinks started.

"Rum?" I said stopping at the liquor cabinet.

"What else?" Nick said.

"Vodka maybe?"

The girls were already to the kitchen where *their* action was taking place now. Duke was lingering on the porch. Later, it will be the dinner table, porch and then back to the living room. It was Amanda's order of things.

"Get real," Sally said stepping out of the kitchen overhearing my vodka joke.

"I know. I'm just yanking the chain a little. Rum it is."

This was going to be more fun than Amanda and Lizzy could have imagined. And all for Duke—just to introduce him to us as her semiofficial significant other. I knew that I would be seeing Duke many more times and at the parties in the city too. What fun he must be having, getting a shit-load of us "old-timers" at the lake on Amanda's money, driving Pete's Duce.

I handed the drinks to Sally and Nick.

"Here we are . . . the man who wears the star. I'm taking orders," I said to the rest of them.

Nick and Sally savored their drinks immediately. Duke had a beer from the fridge, and Lizzy and Amanda already had poured themselves white wine. Everyone wanted tons of answers to so many questions to be asked. I was sipping my vodka in comfort, for I didn't need to be the lead pony.

"Where are you from?" Nick asked Duke.

Right there, I could kiss the lord for not asking Duke more questions on the court earlier. Those answers are now coming from another's questions, and I won't have to live with Amanda's wrath later. No way baby, I'll just leave that to the Whinstners to be first on this one!

"East Aurora," Duke said.

My eyes were open on that one, for that's where that new golf course is where I found Michael and his girlfriend first! Better thought and not said I decided.

East Aurora is a fabulous village in the South towns of Western New York—truly a historic, bohemian tourist town—again, after money swallowed its decaying buildings and streets. Before that, it was known as a historic stop on the underground railroad routes, sixties artist community, and hilly farmlands. There still are a few farms soon to be bought out and developed into another golf course community or luxury suburban-type neighborhoods. Twain was right—golf courses are a good waste of a "walk in the woods."

"Eagle Sticks is there, isn't it? It should be pretty well established now," I said making conversation with Duke.

"I've played since it first opened . . . It's in great shape. I live right down the road."

"We own one of the lots on nine," Nick said.

I went to my station to refresh Nick and Sally's cocktails, thinking how great it was not being first to ask personal questions of Duke. Apparently, he was in equipment sales, loved golf, and he and Amanda were becoming very close. She was determined to introduce Duke and have overlapping associates to carry on her parties at the lake. Its Amanda's little twist on chosen guests to mix with Lizzy and me I'm sure.

However, Nick, Sally and I didn't have any lulls in conversations, reminiscing on our past fun before anyone was ever married. Mostly, it's the crazy things we talked about from our childhood days. Amanda, Lizzy and Duke would just listen, laugh too or shake their head in amazement to the stories we told. Amanda was mostly the "head shaker." Lizzy knows I've had a wild side.

Everybody got to know each other that evening. And at the end of the party, we agreed that we'd do it again, together, sometime this season. It was good to see Nick and Sally. Amanda's party was a success, and Duke was staying for the rest of the weekend.

The Whinstners said their thanks—an acknowledgement for another get-together, and drove the several miles down the road to their home.

I still had my questions tonight to ask Lizzy about Duke after we all retired to the privacy of our rooms.

"How'd you like the Whinstners?" I said, folding the bed sheets back. "Some old friends, aren't they?"

"Yep, it was a good mix of people for Duke to meet."

"True."

"True about Amanda and Duke being an item now."

"That's really not for publication yet."

"That's cool, but what's the whole story here?"

"Like what . . ." Lizzy said delaying an obvious full disclosure.

"Do you think I'm stupid? He has a tan line around his marriage finger. Must be from golf."

"He has to be more careful with that."

"Ha!" I jumped in now knowing that Duke is married!

"Amanda has another married man!" I could only say, "And you knew him before tonight too. Didn't you?"

"Well, I didn't want to tell you for nobody was to know before us tonight . . . and your friends. They are nice people."

"Don't go changing the subject here—he's married. Like Pete. That concerns me a little, doesn't it you?"

"I can't tell her what to do."

"Well, somebody should. This will be her second spouse of someone else's she's doing. I don't like it, and I know she's our friend and all, but that's wrong to have another family waiting somewhere. You know how Kim felt and that poor wife and kids of Peter's."

"This is different."

"Because of her money? I don't think so. You'll have to explain that one to me."

"She's been lonely and was an only child. I've known her for a long time."

"Why, because no one had her money. That's still a damn poor excuse," I said in a lighter tone to make the rest of the evening ours, instead of this conversation about Amanda and the new Duke.

We were going to bed happily. And that was more than enough information to share for now. For as already famously said, "tomorrow's another day," and I damn well wanted to wake up happy. My last unspoken thought before sleep though was that Amanda is a "spouse stealer," and I was hoping not to dream about it.

I thought about Duke playing golf where Michael had his affair—and did Amanda know more . . . *first* before me, thus making me *second?* Only guesses, but Duke and Amanda maybe already knew for there was one other couple ahead of Michael on the course that day, quite a bit further in play, after the first nine holes. How many times have they played this course anyway? Through Lizzy, Amanda gave me those golf vouchers for me to use with my editor! Did Amanda know first?

Closing my eyes for the night, I could only wonder if this was a setup for me being the first to tell of Michael's affair!

# CHAPTER TWELVE

# *The Spinning*

I T WAS A great sailing season with breezy afternoons and calm seas in the early mornings and dusk. I must have sailed as much as power-boated so far this year. Sailing's a gas but you have to keep changing sides of the boat all the time. I'm much more of a deckchair or throttling-the-controls sailor. The wind in my hair this summer was just fine on either vessel. It was the lake, and we all looked forward to opening the houses every spring, making them ready for summer living and getting tanned in the sun. Buffalo has its seasons so you need to make the best of them.

Simply, at this age, the fact is that I'm a "permanent" visitor-in-residence. I would stay at Nick's parents' house when I was in high school and college; and before that, at ReKouk's with a buddy named Steffen in junior high and before. They were good people too, most of them, most of the time. As time slipped by, we all played musical houses and sometimes would see each other from a shoreline distance, having morning coffee by the lake, raising our cups toasting the day.

Nick and Sally knew my first and second wives socially, and those were good times, at least until the divorces. They both had a bit of family money and always accepted me graciously at the lake., with the now-seemingly short estrangement from their friendship.

These are good times too, with Lizzy. I'm in love with her more than anything that I can ever remember having loved that much before. She is my friend to share dreams with. I trust her, and she is a part of my soul. We feel the same about each other, sharing most of everything so that we could always sleep comfortably at night, awakening in the morning to smile again.

The Whinstners coordinated our next party and were bringing their thirty-four-foot sloop over to Amanda's beach house. It was a day of sailing. They would moor in deeper water for the keel's draft in front of Amanda's beach. It was our very next major outing with Duke and Amanda this summer. Amanda agreed because we all had gotten along so well when she first introduced Duke to the lake. I had her rubber dingy primed and ready and beached by 7:30 a.m.

The others were just getting up, starting breakfast and packing our lunch before the day of sailing at noon. Noon was a good time to have the Whinstners moor off of Amanda's shoreline, for it'd take an hour before we could set sail again, making sure everything was on board and secured before getting underway. Shortly, we'll all be aboard.

Having come-about, heading toward the Buffalo skyline, the wind picked up and started gusting by the time we were mid lake. Nick and Sally loved "pushing the limits" of a good wind before returning to port. They both are great sailors—heavy rum drinkers though, so I made sure we had a good mix of drinks to be had at lunch. Rum, beer and vodka . . . is there anything else one drinks while sailing? Yes! Since we were motoring out in calm winds, Bloodys would be first; I already made the mix the night before. All you have to do is shake and chill before serving. It was a good patch ready to shake and serve as the first drink on our day of sailing.

The weather was perfectly warm, with sun predicted all day. Lake Erie is not a lake to mess with when the weather's hostile while boating. We all remembered the story of the sinking of Edmund Fitzgerald. At the lake, we do not play with the devil just for devil's play, at least not anymore at our age.

Duke was a golfer and definitely not a sailor, so I kept my eye on him as a personal quest, for he could get hit with a shifting boom or tied in a sheet as we came about if he didn't move readily with the boat. Sailing's not for everyone, at least not all the time, for real sailors move with the boat and the waves coming at you. Non-sailors are always to be watched, and knowing the difference, I kept watch over Duke. Amanda was Lizzy's chore. And who wants to come about to pick up an overboard sailor, I ask you? If it happened to be Duke, Amanda would have to sit down, shut up, and listen to us sailors bringing the boat around just to save his life, knowing he had a few cocktails in him, and if not, I'd hog tie her as Nicky called the orders! I kept a guarding eye every time we tacked into the afternoon wind.

We sailed around Point Breeze—that jetted out into the lake where its distant west shores were always calm to anchor for lunch, swimming and water games. The girls even brought their blankets to sun on in front of the tall shoreline sand dunes. It was always hot as an oven to lie there. The west shores were mostly protected coves on that side of the Point. Nicky and I would always lead the "men" to the top of the sand dunes like warriors and then run down tumbling when we were kids; but, if now, more as half-drunken adults. The fun was the same.

Securely anchored on the shores west of Point Breeze, we drank the end of the Bloodys. We always eat well too, especially with the best basket presentations that Amanda and Lizzy created. Amanda did her Martha Stewart stuff, and Lizzy coordinated the presentation like Sandra Dee.

I was determined to get all three of us men on top of that dune today and then come down anyway you wanted. Nick and I already challenged each other to who would fall faster and further. We both felt like kids again, and the competition for us would always be there to share, forever. The Duke could slip down just as long as he got down. Hell, the climb to the top is what will kill you. Duke played golf three or four rounds a week, so he should make it. He'll just have to come down slowly, for he couldn't do what Nick and I were challenging.

The moment of truth will be after lunch when everyone is in his or her suits on shore. That's when our aging fat hangs out individually to be seen by the group. And sticky buns—it's hard to understand their effect on you over the years, especially if you eat them as much as Amanda did; at the moment of truth, our suits will show everything. The Duke was stocky, Lizzy looked great, the Whinstners always looked the same, and I was pretty much tight from all the tennis but a bit punchy in the stomach for living a good life. The drinking has its part I'm sure.

"Not cold," I said dropping off the bow into the water.

I looked up to the rail, expecting the first download of towels and such wrapped tightly to keep them dry. Duke handed down a full gym bag and then another and that was enough, so I turned toward shore. I could hear beer bottles clinking in one of them as I adjusted it on my shoulder. Lizzy was next to slip in with a bag held over her head. She's a trooper! Everyone followed with something except Amanda.

Once everyone was waist deep in the lake, Amanda decided she'd stay with the boat, and from her tone, you could tell there was no reason to change her mind. We were going ashore for more sun and fun, Nick, Sally and I knew that—Lizzy too, who was here once before, when I showed her the secret path through the woods, but it's Duke who was going to be *christened* to the west shore sand dunes.

When Nick finally hit the shore, having waded through the waters quickly, he dropped his bag and started running toward the dunes. I was already standing thirty feet in front of him when he hit the sand; he knew I was given a head start for a race to the top if I took the bait. I was older but had that distance on him and took off too. After we were both knee-deep in the steep sand, we slowed down dramatically, and my distance seemed not so great at all. He was close enough behind me now, and we were breathing like athletes on a course at the finish line. When he was close enough, he grabbed my foot to slow me down, coming alongside me. I thought fair is fair, so I pushed him sideways, knocking him down onto his butt. I had the distance again and was not using any more tricks other than that one, which he started. We hit the top almost at the same time. His younger age made him stronger than I am.

"It's a draw," I said, knowing full well I could claim honors without tricks, but he would challenge that as a matter of interpretation anyway, especially since he gave me the head start.

"Shit, I haven't done this in ages," he said out-of-breath.

"Me neither . . . and longer than you."

"You wild man, it's good to see you."

"Likewise. I haven't seen Sally for so long, she looks exactly the same."

"Thanks, buddy."

"Hey . . . after this, let's do tennis. You're still playing?"

"Let's race down for a beer."

"In a minute," I said still catching my breath.

We then both sat down on the hill top, still breathing hard and both knew that our friendship had many more years before we died.

We watched the girls fuss with the towels and unpacking, and he challenged a guess which gym bag had the beer. I brought them ashore so I took the challenge. We were almost ready to take the plunge into the deep, downward sand at full speed, knowing full well that we'd lose our footing and have to dive into the rolls like kids before standing on our feet. Everything Nick and I did growing up was a challenge, just for the game and to make everything we did fun. And fun is the name of the game, being at the Point with old friends—new ones too of course. My wife made me happier than I've ever been, if not only for today.

The sun was so warm that Nick and I were ready to take off but saw Duke halfway into climbing the dune. We decided to wait for him to get two thirds of the way as our starting gun. We tore out a clump of sawgrass growing on Nick's right to drop. And then we waited some more, for Duke was not making any progress in his climb. He was in slow motion, breathing heavily. Nick and I simply sat longer, looking at the lake and his anchored boat. We could see that Amanda was sunbathing in the cockpit lounge.

"She's a character," I said, still looking out.

"Very strange to understand, we really don't see her much, other than sailing by her house."

"She came with Lizzy and a few others . . . Have you met Kim?"

"Once. That one is very distant. We met her at a fundraiser in the city once."

"She belongs to a lot of clubs and participates at mostly none, but she's Lizzy's good friend, so I go along with most of her crazed stuff."

"What's his name is almost here . . . what's his name?"

"Duke, short for Doug. Are your ready?"

"When you are."

Duke was weaving hard now and almost to the "line in the sand."

"Get ready buddy-boy, for I'm going to beat your ass to the beer!"

"Right!" Nick said, challenging me again as he dropped the sawgrass without warning.

We leaped down that hill, passing Duke who turned his head to watch a finish line he just now understood. It was a tie, but I let Nick crack the first beer, which I handed to him, having unzipped the bag already. I felt healthy in mind and body, for that kind of racing would kill anyone over forty-five.

MARK FRANCIS SCHWAB

The girls were lying on their beach towels in the hot sand, and you could see they were in heaven with the heat. It took Duke a bit to get down, several more minutes at least, but he shortly joined us. There were no beach chairs so he sat down hard on one of the blankets where the beer was. We gave him a cold beer, and his eyes smiled without saying a word, not even thanks. To Nicky and I, friends didn't always need to say please and thanks. I was really starting to like this guy, The Duke. He was a happy and harmless person that would try something as weird as climbing to the top of the dunes, but we all knew he would be more comfortable in a golf cart. He would have to volley though, for he does have a racket—always in the back of his car. I wondered if Amanda had something to do with that. But today, he really needed water not beer in this hot sun. He'd have to get that back to the boat, for I only brought cold beer to shore! The girls only had beer also. Sally could last as long as Nick with just beer, but we were all together, with Amanda on his boat.

"Hot enough for you ladies?" I quipped starting a second beer.

We sat there for another fifteen minutes with little conversation, for it was the lake and sand we sailed here to see. And that's all we really wanted to feel: tranquility, meeting of the mind and soul, friends and silence to reflect singularly yet sharing the moments. Who could ask for anything better than sharing this blissful contentment in life?

I looked over to the boat and Amanda was now set with her feet dangling over the bow, watching us on shore. She was eating something. We did bring some sticky buns for desert, and I assumed it's one of those. She looked big from the shore.

"Let's go in for more lunch," Lizzy said.

Everyone agreed, and we started to pack the bags. The air was hot, the few beers left were warm and the lake would be refreshing. I took the two gym bags and waded into the water. Amanda saw us coming, went to the stern and got a wrap to cover her waist and legs as she return to the bow, watching us again. When we reached the boat she took the bags from us. Sally, Duke and Liz climbed the ladder, and Nick and I decided to swim around the boat for a bit. It was a pleasant temperature in the chest-high waters. I could only think how really good it was, swimming at the Point again with Nick and Sally again. We always had fun at this "secret" beach and sand dunes, which you could only get to by boat, unless you knew the hidden path through the woods I showed Liz that one summer.

Duke threw out a football, hitting the waters between Nicky and me, and the game was on. The three of us played for a bit, returning it to Duke to throw the long ball from his perch on the stern. You could see that Amanda and the girls were happy about this too.

Amanda did a good thing that evening with her dinner party guest list, for Nick and I didn't even remember what drew us apart anymore. It was insignificant stuff now, and as far as I knew, my first wife moved to Hawaii or somewhere tropical, and they haven't seen her since either. Her family still had houses up here, but nobody ever saw them either, not even at the Lake Club's parties.

The girls had fun directing Duke where to throw the football and to whom. They got into it a bit, challenging how far we could dive to catch it, but I was now tiring and told Nick so. We had our fun on the dunes and agreed to go up for snacks and a few more cold ones. I know I needed one, for I was puffing harder than climbing the hill.

I certainly will feel some muscle pain tomorrow or for the next few days, and at this age, it was anyone's guess. I'm sure Lizzy will confer when I start to complain. But today is today, and everyone was having fun in the sun, sailing together.

We pulled anchor and stared to raise the main sail to come about. In the hands of a good captain, I didn't mind changing sides of the boat, for Nick would tack longer for our comfort to get us home—the wind is his power, moving us forward.

Amanda had an itch to get Duke home. She was securing everything on board that made it obvious that we were going to be on land soon, and nobody said anything. She had her signs that most of us could read by now, but I always let someone else ask the questions first.

The Whinstners instinctively knew this too, and it felt good sharing such a hard thought about our friend's controlling behavior, for we also were sharing our renewed friendship together again on his boat, and you could read Amanda like a book. Money does not make the person, but with enough you could buy someone, and I knew that would never happen to Lizzy and me to live that way. We all wanted the money—trust me on this one. Amanda simply had more than everyone else.

It is man's age-old dream to be the greatest of philanthropist, even when you only could share just beyond your dollar's boundaries.

Philanthropy, no matter how small, was good enough to feel good about yourself. It has so much chemistry just to say it; yet it is an emotional issue we can only answer from within and as much as we can share for our graces to have more than enough to give. I love the thought, lest being able to make such gifts with any extra money, and Lizzy and I did what we felt we should.

Nicky kept most of his money close to his vest, but if there was something for helping dogs, like we all had at some point growing up, I know he'd give any amount of money to save a dog in distress. That's why he and Sally were still together and never divorced, for they respected their marriage vows and loved their life and animals. They would help any way they could that way. They took a great liking to Lizzy and me as a team.

We drifted just off shore to Amanda's where the rubber dingy was moored and waiting. I got the landing party in the little craft with our bags and motored to shore. Duke was saying something about a nice day with nice people. I could see why he thought this. I beached our dingy, tilting the motor as we hit, so everyone could get out dry. The Whinstners stayed until we all hit shore before setting sail back to their Lake Club mooring.

The sun, the wind and the booze—not to mention the exercise—has a way of knocking you out. Of course, beer and sun do the same thing on any outing, land or sea. Add vodka and rum and you're dead tired. I told the group I needed a nap and went upstairs to lie down for a while. Lizzy came up after I was comfortably relaxing on the bed, and we had great sex. I could see tan lines on her body from today, and it turned me on greatly. I love sex with my wife. A good hug always followed no matter how fast anyone came, and a soft kiss on the cheek meant everything.

"Your friends are very nice, Jon."

"I've known them for a long time, and then things drifted apart after my earlier divorces. We've talked but never really stayed in touch like we used to. I love them a lot, but they were on the other side then."

"They seem to like me too."

"Nicky and I always made a game of everything to compete at, that's why."

"They're very generous and nice. I love their boat."

"This is boating country. Duke looked like he had fun."

"How do you like him?"

"It's early, but he's gentle enough. Had a hard time with the dunes though. You gotta' stay in shape, and he was puffing very hard. I didn't think he'd make it back to the boat."

"He plays a lot of golf."

"Let's not forget about that tan line on his finger. Where are his people?" I could only ask.

Lizzy knew where I was going, so she didn't say a thing. She rolled over and hugged me as her husband, and that was just fine with me to stop talking and simply nap together.

Cocktails and dinner would be here very soon, and I knew I would keep looking at Duke's untanned marriage band, knowing there was a family somewhere that didn't have a daddy at home. And this would be my next question: does he have kids too? I'm getting the feeling he does. And right now, that's not a question to have answered as I held Lizzy in my arms.

The lake, love and cocktails do wonderful things to comfort a man's soul. And if I wasn't the *first* to fix cocktails, they'd all have to wait. Usually nobody made them but me when at Amanda's, other than her open bottle of wine she kept in the Fridge. She would always pour hers unannounced first, rather then her guests', even if they wanted to imbibe sooner. She never would open something fresh until the last drop was gone, stale or not. Amanda, Duke, Lizzy and I made it an early evening after our dinner since we all had too much fun in the sun already.

It was another sunny, warm day, and I was up at sunrise. I love the lake's sunrise alone—anywhere really, but at the lake, it seemed more than life itself, being outside with a cup of coffee by yourself. I can't resist being the first to rise in the morning with all that time you have alone before the sleepers awake. It's a magical hour of the day, seeing the sunrise. Its mystical reflections from the lake's surface shine deep into your heart.

I still had my questions from the night before that I wanted to know and will have them answered soon, even if it would be bedtime again until answered. Men need to get real answers to real questions about real things happening in a shared life, and Lizzy will "fess-up" when asked directly, and that wasn't needed just yet.

I made fresh ground coffee this morning. I love to drink strong, fresh ground coffee every morning. Amanda hated when I made coffee first, for she always said it was too strong. I don't like drinking hot colored water, and this morning, I was in the kitchen first, with no controls or directions. I made it to my strength, not something I had to drink because Amanda got there first and made it too weak. Nobody was up, so she could make another pot later after I had half of this one.

Standing barefoot on the dewed grass at the water's edge, I heard stirring on the upper floor through the open windows and knew someone would be down shortly, so I took a big swallow, went back into the house and refilled my cup and walked to the porch to sit alone in one of the chairs facing at the lake. I could hear Duke and Amanda speaking in the kitchen. Amanda was getting breakfast started, and Duke came out on the porch to join me.

"Good coffee," he said.

"I made it earlier, before you got up."

"Amanda doesn't like strong coffee."

"Yes, I know. Sorry, but I got there first. Let's get another cup before she pours it out. If we're lucky, we can finish the pot . . . and don't tell her I said that."

"Not from me," Duke said as we went into the house, which smelled like cinnamon and sugar-baked pastries now.

Lizzy was down too and was busy making some breaded-egg dish with bacon on top. It was going to be another feast for us "beach people." One thing was for sure, I was going to make Duke play a round of tennis just to work off all of these calories we were consuming. And we'd consume a round or two of Bloodys just a bit after breakfast.

It was toward the end of the weekend, and we'd all be heading back to the city that afternoon, and Duke would be back in East Aurora for his games of golf at Eagle Sticks for the week. Amanda certainly took care of him, just like she did Pete.

We had those Bloodys an hour or so after breakfast, then Duke and I hit the courts. We had a good volley going, but Duke was breathing hard again, like he did a third of the way up the dunes yesterday.

"You want to break for water?" I asked him.

"No . . . in a bit though. I'm not as young as before."

"Who is?" I half laughed with a concerning eye on him.

"I'm good—just sometimes get more tired than others."

"We'll go easy, okay?"

"Good, I'll catch my breath."

"You better, I don't want to be blowing air down your throat and pounding on your sorry-ass chest."

"Not to worry. I'm fine."

"That's what we all say. Let's stop and get some water."

We went to the cooler next to the bench and sat down. I gave him water, and I had beer. We stocked the cooler daily each weekend, making sure we always kept our supplies on ice prior to playing. I could tell he was really out of shape for lack of continuous exercise, especially after seeing him climbing in the deep sand. And since we were sharing "sacred" moments alone, I wanted to get a few more questions answered.

"Tell me, where's the wife? Any kids?"

"How'd you know?"

"Your finger has a missing-ring tan line—not all in the right places, Duke. And we don't hide much once everyone's on board. How about kids? Have any?"

"Three. We don't get along well, so I've changed venues a little."

"The wife or the kids?" I asked.

I was going to get more information at this point. This needed clarifying for I don't like late-night questions of this sort given to Lizzy in bed.

"I love the kids. It's the wife. We don't agree anymore. They're in junior high."

"Is she aware of this . . . at the beach and things?"

"I think so. She doesn't seem to care where I go or when I'm back."

"That's a problem. So golf sometime down at Eagle Sticks?" I said to change the subject.

"Of course . . . tomorrow. I can get you guest passes."

"Not tomorrow, but sometime this week could be good. You can get passes?"

"Get them for you anytime. I'm chartered—Amanda arranged that."

"Amanda gave me passes to play with my editor when it opened."

"I know."

"What else do you know about that course?" I said trying to put two and two together with answers.

"Everything's for sale and I know the best properties," Duke said.

"How about who's played there and when?"

"Been there since the beginning . . . seen just about everybody who's ever played since it opened."

"Really, just about everybody?" I had to ask.

"Yep, just about everybody."

"Tell me then, is it mostly twosomes, foursomes, you know . . . maybe couples and stuff?"

"Sure . . . that's where Amanda and I would play before meeting you guys here at the beach."

"No shit. Do you remember other couples who played in front or behind you?"

"Sometimes, maybe some. Amanda knew everyone, but we didn't talk to anyone because of my wife and all."

"I understand. She must have recognized a few she mentioned to you, I guess. So it's a bit of a couple's thing out there?"

"Oh ya, Amanda knows everyone. She know who's there, but we don't socialize or anything."

"I understand," is all I could say thinking about how I found Michael there with his girlfriend. And I wasn't sure how to ask my next questions but knew they were going to be asked.

"Did you see other couples out there . . . like you with Amanda privately dating?" I couldn't help being blunt about it.

"Sure . . . it's a hideaway still, for nobody's there, but the weekends are getting full."

"Yes, nothing like a full weekend. So you saw other couples playing during the week, like being alone . . . together?"

"There was one couple Amanda said something about a couple of times, but she never said anything to them . . . just that she knew them. We were always hanging back to ourselves."

"I can see why . . . you're still being married. Did she say anything about them?"

"Just that she was very surprised at someone for having someone with them."

Boy, did that hit hard. Was I set up so long ago to be the first to tell about Michael and his affair? It certainly began to look that way. And it didn't set well with me. Amanda could be controlling with her own stuff, around her own property and all, but if she set me up for that, that is evil, manipulative and the work of the devil. She used me to be first when I was really second. And here she is, with another married man!

"You do know about Pete, don't you?"

We didn't volley anymore after our conversation, which became just filler after that. We had a basic understanding now and liked each other enough that I knew Duke would be there from now on. We could gesture about having his skeletons out of the bag, secretly held by us, at Amanda's or our parties, without having to speak of them again. Duke was permanently added to the group who has fun at the beach; and everyone knew Amanda has stolen him for her personal pleasure with her money and Pete's Buick. I hope to god that I never meet his family left behind like I did Pete's. And everyone now knew she had backed herself up while Pete was alive. There is no doubt about it: *Amanda is a serial spouse stealer.*

"What in the hell kind of person is this?" is all I could ask if I was to ask someone.

# CHAPTER THIRTEEN

# *Pieces to the Puzzle*

A COUPLE OF weeks were to pass by in the city before heading up to the beach houses again. Amanda and Duke were off at some famous golf resort in the southeastern states, North Carolina I think. It was one of those PGA tour courses that everyone wanted to play and was very expensive. But since Duke was the big golfer and Amanda was paying for everything, it would hardly dent her pocketbook, continuing to encase him. Lizzy and I rarely ever went on vacation just to play golf anymore. If the resort didn't have "everything," we simply wouldn't plan just a golf trip. Duke must be beyond returning to his home and family by now, having his life purchased by Amanda and Pete's Buick; his wife was either happy about it or wanted to kill him. She must have been given some settlement, for nobody ever talked about it at this point, knowing how Amanda chooses and closes her deals.

In the meantime, Lizzy and I had scheduled a party at our house for it was our turn again to have something in the city. And quite frankly, I don't think Amanda was ready for something that big in the city yet for The Duke to be introduced to *everyone*, so they were noticeably absent.

Our party had the usual city crowd, but I decided to invite the Whinstners even though it was still summer and they'd have to drive across the Peace Bridge into the suburbs. They hadn't been to our new place, and it's the least I could do for such a fine day of sailing and fun at the dunes with them. They knew some of the people too, so I didn't worry about anything other than Kim wanting my bartender's spot in the kitchen. She was coming all right and without Michael for he wasn't invited. She had dated a few people since her divorce, and Lizzy and I had met both—or was it three now? I just don't remember, but she was bringing Fred, her new *nice* guy. I liked Fred but knew that it wasn't a match—just great sex and *instant* companionship for Kim. Fred, I'm sure, didn't wish it that way—just sex and companionship—but would take as much as he could keep, keeping it going and hoping it'd never end. I liked Fred but knew what she was up to. He never saw it coming and probably will never see it go. He'll know only when she's left, relatively early on, and have just the memory of wild sexual fun gone by the way side.

I could hardly wait for our party to start. Freddie loved Kim's poofed hair dances, and she loved his attention. Now that I had seen the other side of all of our friendships—Kim's dances, Freddie's drool and with Michael now so far in the distance—this was going to be fun again. And hell, let her be bartender, for I had the Whinstners there as old, regained friends that I could spend time with.

We had the kids as helpers again, but they weren't kids anymore; they were in college and wanted the money. They loved our money, for we set prices well and tipped even better. That was a bit of our philanthropy too, making sure our friends' children had enough to go through college expenses with some extra perks—those kind of cash perks that one could waste on pizza and booze, being able to pay for everyone's night of fun. I loved helping young scholars needing a breather while learning their chosen discipline of study. We all expected their grades to be exemplary, for they were an extension of us. And a "given" gift is a gift to keep forever, especially when you're young, needing money on your own, studying at some distant college. Thank god these grown kids weren't near marriage yet—just doing their college sex. I wish them much luck as they spend their earned money. They probably were having as much fun as we were, just watching and serving us! College kids on a roll.

Most of the guests had arrived, *and we were on a roll.* The Whinstners and their guest haven't yet, but they had to cross the border and I knew they would be here sometime soon.

Kimmie was flaming through the room with Freddie in tow, telling all of her tales. Her limits weren't even matched yet, with this younger stud. She smiled like a shtupped woman only can, and her eyes were bragging to every conversation they bounced to and from. No "poofed" dances yet, but that was sure to come. I had more time now to talk to our guests because the "help" was helping me bartend. I'm sure they could make more "exotic" drinks than anything I knew of anyway. I knew that I could plant a seed in Freddie to see Kim's "poof dancing" sooner than later.

The Whinstners arrived with their friend Lenord, or Lee as we called him, who I knew but haven't seen since when we were kids. I knew he existed all this time, but his money was another league altogether like Amanda's in so many ways, and he was not the sharpest knife in the drawer by any means. I always thought of him as "stupid as stupid can" be on roller skates . . ., and we never fucked around in front of his rich parents, who, by the way, were dead for several years now and left him an industrial company's parachute even Amanda would want. Dumb as rocks and rich as hell. And now, Lee just stepped back into my life after so many years, with the Whinstners. Back then, Lee could only come out to play once in a while into "the challenges of the children." If his parents knew what we were up, they would have killed him—or us—every time. So here's Lee standing in my house like a rock, not saying anything other than to answer a question asked to him. He was like a mime in a park who would move slightly to the right and then to the left. He was so shy but understood the topic and actually could offer an answer, coherently. That's the Lee I remember: the same preppy clothes only a much bigger fit to his now-huge frame. He still had his simple messages to say at timeless points about meaningless historic topics, which he knew by heart. He was usually right though once he did say something meaningful.

We were older now, so I give him my full graces for still looking normal, living in his parent's beach estate still. And what a house! His private clay courts were always groomed by the help daily. They'd brush and water them to perfection. I have no idea who he was playing with or if they were ever used since I was fourteen. Nicky and Lee were friends as long as anyone at the beach. Good old Lee. I always liked him, as little as he could come out and play.

I walked through the party and guest-filled rooms like an owner of a restaurant. The kids watched me too, making sure someone I pointed to for another drink would be immediately served, for no one was ever denied anything at our parties, even if they didn't ask for it. These were grown kids, and they enjoyed seeing us getting drunk as much as they did becoming drinking adults. We always had someone who could drive you home, or you would simply spend the night in one of the guest rooms. That was the law if you needed it and we saw to it. No drunk driving—that was my rule, and that was what the gated beach houses were for across the border. You could always walk the shoreline or private roadway home or talk to the security guard that made you leave your car and drive you home. Here in the city, we allowed no bad driving after multiple cocktails. It was everyone's job too, at least to point it out so that I could make the recommended choice of staying here. We had three extra bedrooms, and I'd simply take their keys. No dummies behind the wheel, and bless Lee who would only drink beer and have only two or three at that—not like the rest of us who loved vodka, rum or "crushed ice" in our single malt scotch.

In fact, I can't recall Lee having more than three beers ever but definitely a couple on the dunes as kids when we stole our parent's supplies to get away and be wildly trying to mimic the adults who taught us how to captain a sail or powerboat. Lee's dad would kill you if he even heard of our outings at the dunes. He controlled Lee's childhood life, and nobody messed with Lee's dad. Lee was harmless and gentle, much like Duke is today.

The party was a total gas. I enjoyed following behind Kimmie and Fred as they pranced from group to group. She'd drag him in and take over the conversation as if there wasn't one going on already. Fred would just nod yes to her imposed sexual acts that she'd unabashedly describe. This was almost an *instant addiction*, if life were instant, and this was as instant as it was going to get, at least for Freddie—just not real for either of them. That's our party crew for you, *instantly* a game to win for its challenge alone. I'd look back at Lee, who was standing with Nick and Sally smiling emphatically. Kimmie was going to "poof" soon, and I wanted to see it again.

"Freddie, my boy, how's the life hanging?"

"So great, man. Nice party. You have everything here."

"Thanks. I try as much as I can afford."

"You . . . you have it all."

"Not all of it Freddie . . . I work hard to enjoy entertaining our friends with style."

"Kim is hot tonight."

"Damn right she is. Have the girls been to the bathroom yet?"

"What? Talking?"

"Yes. They don't pee. They gossip!"

"Did you hear something?"

"Nothing at all, other than you two doing the thing . . . a lot."

"Yea. She's good sex. Good sex . . . I hope she likes me."

"Damn right she does, she loves it too. Why would you be here? You're a lucky man tonight and you know it."

"Darn right," Freddie said, as I left him hinting with an okay for her "poof dance" by pushing up the hair on the back of my head.

His eyes were wide open like those of children waiting for candy, hoping he could make that happen. I gently fluffed Kim's hair as I walked by her into another room full of guests.

We were going strongly, and everyone looked happy and full of life that I knew we had a hit for a party. The kind of evening where the guests never wanted it to end or anyone to leave. There was always one last couple talking on and on who were just a street or two over where they could walk home. They never did though, and this is where I broke the rule for no drinking and walking home. If it was longer than a par five hole in golf you'd have to stay. Two or three of our friends fit in this category for late night, after the partying at our home. Hell, if they'd stay, we'd all have a late-night hot tub under the stars and some kind of brunch when we got up, with leftovers invented by me of course. The other male of the group would be in charge of making the Bloodys in the morning.

The music got louder by someone stirring the crowd, having found my CD collection and picked a hot eighties tune made by a sixties artist: Aretha Franklin's *Pink Cadillac*, or was it called *Driving Down the Freeway*? I couldn't remember, but I saw that the controls were in the hands of none other than Kim and Freddie, and they were jiving at their new station, making the group more than interested to start bopping too. The party was going to another level with everyone dancing around the room to their levels of intoxication and blaring music. Freddie was reading the titles, and Kim was picking the songs that drove the frenzy. It'd be only a matter of time before the "poof dance," and I couldn't see it soon enough!

Lizzy and I loved it all and knew we'd never be the Joneses chasing inherited money, but these are our friends in this circle, and not everyone with Lee's or Amanda's money was here. And to tell the truth, I don't think I'd want that responsibility handed to me, although the perks sure would be nice, but the pain somewhere would make you crazy I'm sure, like Duke driving Pete's Buick.

*Instant everything for nothing.* That's out of the park for Lizzy and me and for most of us here tonight. That's not to say there wasn't good family business with lots of money for sailboats, country clubs and the Lake Club. This is our life: comfortably fun, in excess most of the time, and almost wanting for nothing, except for it to always continue. If life stayed right here, at this moment, for the rest of my life, I'd be a very happy camper and then simply die at an old age, *instantly* I hope. I'm just an aging guy that agreed with the sixties good "sex, drugs and rock and roll . . . and make love not war." I think we all did, except our guest's kids who are still working as the paid help. They were getting a whole new world view on their own just watching us.

# CHAPTER FOURTEEN

# *Movable Feasts*

M ICHAEL DIED FROM a highway crash involving drunk drivers—I'm sure he was drunk too—at least that's the story, and sadness was all around us now. Apparently, it wasn't his fault, but if you're driving drunk you're drunk, and I don't drive drunk. Kim was a mess and over to our house in the city almost daily. I found myself repeating certain positive points to her, not that she didn't remember them, but because she wanted to hear them again and again. I always tried to make them sound fresh and poignant, making any positive reference I could relate it to. She was imbibing as many comparisons as I could make up and hand her.

Death really hurts when you've known the person for a long time, not to mention being married to them. Lizzy and I gave our hearts to Kim in her time of reflection and pain. Their kids were grown now, and I really don't see them other than Christmas and such holidays. But Kimmie needed stories related to her now, and Liz and I did our best to bring up all of her bows she has been with, and I kept mentioning Freddie for her last man-in-hand.

Amanda was home with Duke now from their extended vacation, and our next party was scheduled back at her beach house soon. From what Lizzy said, they had a really good time golfing and were ready for more exposure to the group thing. Duke was always going to be around, and that was that—newly un-suntanned marriage finger and all. We all felt happy about this—for Amanda's companionship and all being out in the open now.

Pete's Buick still haunts me though as "over-gifting," much like she controlled Pete with all the trimmings, but Duke didn't really care anyway, with all the golf vacations, he was oblivious, content, smiling and playing tennis with me occasionally. And that was enough for me not to question how she paid off his marriage, but I had my eye on Amanda's methods—bar nothing. They are highly unethical and are totally selfish to say the least, no matter how much money you have. Buying people's affection is simply a sick thing to do. There is a mad method of psychosis here—one that cannot be overlooked or condoned for getting her mate.

One does not just pick someone, and then buy their life and emotions through clothes, vacations or Buicks, especially used Buicks. And you do not pay their spouse's off either just to make them go away with expenses covered, although I'm sure that helped in her closure to a messy situation. Stealing spouses is the work of the devil. Hell, Amanda used her money unsparingly to conquer her loneliness as the devil would grant your last, dying wish for immortality.

At her home this weekend, the *Bloody Brunches* with lavish dinner parties were in full swing, and tonight was no different. The Whinstners and Lee were invited too. Amanda thought this was a gift to me in some sort of a controlling effort for Lizzy's and my trusted affection. Duke liked them too, and Nick and I were gaining old ground, talking about sailing outside of the group, enjoying every minute remembering our old times together. Sally would laugh as she used to at our conversations as kids.

This was *classic* beach time at the lake, and the Whinstners brought Lee with them all the time now—old Lee, who couldn't get out of his own way, spending money on things he was not accustomed to do as a child. Lee needs to get a life, and Nick and Sally were trying to help as his friends, as harmless and helpless as he seemed. I'm not sure he didn't half know it and just acted that way to have his way of the life he's been living forever—alone with the help handling the tennis courts, boats and his dinners.

MARK FRANCIS SCHWAB

I could be jealous too with servants preparing my daily "readiness" to do something, but I wouldn't give up my "brains" for any amount of money. Lee was not the sharpest knife by any means, but he could buy them all, at any time, with his money. I think his parent's metal plating company's parachute came with another five-year SVP title and pay, then he would retain 25 percent of the stock. He had serious money is all one could say. Amanda could be, or is, jealous if they'd compare their millions. I simply don't talk about their money. It was none of my business.

I have enough problems making regular monthly deadlines. Thank god though that I could make my own hours, writing at three in the morning if the thoughts struck me, and Lizzy always gave me her support, knowing I was getting out of bed going to my desk to write my stuff for a living. It was our living and our money. We lived well enough because we both contributed to the pot, and two professional incomes are better than one, especially running with this crew. We wanted for nothing almost, maybe a little more money once in awhile. Like blowing everything off to go to Hawaii. At least, Lee didn't buy his mates on our sailing trips; even when we were kids sailing out of the Lake Club, we would have to bring our own lunches. We did many races then on his parent's boats. Our life was free of wants because of our parent's upbringing, paying for everything. We didn't know the difference then nor cared because we all had fun daily. As children, we knew some parents had more money than others, but we all shared the toys so it didn't make a damn bit of a difference who owned what—except for Lee's courts and boats. Really, the only difference was trying to beat someone who wasn't as smart, agile and faster than you. We learned that when left alone, we could use our parent's toys and not get caught if all were put back from where we got them.

The Whinstners and Lee came to every party now held. Amanda and Lizzy made sure of that. The Duke felt comfortable around them and had his fun too, and that was important for Amanda and Lizzy, making the Duke feel at home. Pete's death was a matter of being, and we all knew when it's over, it's over. The living must go on into different chapters for the future, remembering the past, while making life a "movable feast" as Hemingway tried to finish his last book before his death. And seemingly, this is a "movable feast" we're having at the beach, without worries other than having happy mates to play with. We were sharing the good and bad together no matter what, and Lizzy was my true mate. Amanda insisted on hosting most of the parties this summer at her house though.

Nick and I were on the porch again stomping our feet, laughing so hard about how much fun something we did way back then, and Lee was voicing something we could or could not remember because he thought he was there too, and quite frankly, sometimes he was.

Lee now has a home in my heart too. I just couldn't have a real conversation with him, unless I gave focus to his thought patterns, not losing what the hell he was trying to say so harmlessly—strange but harmless, for he wouldn't say anything bad or even know that his wording usually made an oxymoron when said in our jovial conversations. But no doubt, Lee had one of the best places out by the dunes, at the end of a long road through the woods.

Kimmie pranced out from one of the doors to the porch like a puma showing off, and then she was gone into the house through another door like a visual-ghost. She was having fun all by herself running between the rooms. She was staying tonight in the third bedroom at Amanda's house, which doubled as an office to run her money from. She had an office in both of her houses. Real estate was a big portfolio investment of hers. It was funny to think that Lee had even more money, not to even count his assets. He was one rich son-of-a-bitch. He never was married or had a girlfriend for as long as I can remember.

Lee's eyes were wide open for each of Kim's run-throughs on the porch. He was amazed by this blatant display of her mythical dancing. Her perfume lingered like jasmine in the evening's calm air. I liked it too, but I never needed anything other than sunblock at the beach. And that's just me thinking about being here from the beginning, growing up at the lake. Old Spice was a commercial on TV. Now that I've aged quite a bit, those are good smells too to remember. And for living such a long and happy life, it's great to have those memories.

The porch was the magnet for the owls to hang out tonight, and the bait was Kimmie dancing through as her choice. Lee, Nick and I were fixtures in our chairs with our drinks. We didn't need to go anywhere other than for refills, and we took turns for that. Lee hadn't done a round yet, but I'm sure he saw enough after Kim's dance-throughs that he was next to run inside for cocktails. Nicky and I were watching Lee, thinking that his primary mission was to chase after Kim just to get closer to her stellar performance tonight.

MARK FRANCIS SCHWAB

Lee couldn't wait to be next for getting up for cocktails, and he was watching my ice melt in the glass from the warm summer air. He wanted Nick to be done too, and I could tell he wouldn't wait for Nick's just to go in and spy on Kim. It was "in his eyes" to be in the house.

I thought about letting him wait for Nick to finish, but I decided that Pavlov's dogs should be free to run, and Lee was patiently waiting his turn.

"I'm ready, you Nicky?"

"No, I'm still driving," Nick laughed.

"Fabulous. Lenord, I'm ready."

"I'll get it!"

"Thanks, my friend. Pour it stiff, and squeeze the lemon please."

"I will. That's Kim, right? I mean she is . . ." he could only say.

"Yes, and watch her for me too," I said.

Nick and I looked at each other smiling because we knew Lee had a "hard-on" for this woman now. Simply, we liked the thought that Lee was excited enough about something he wanted to do by himself. We grinned shaking our heads, not saying a word. We just knew Lee was acting on a real impulse, and at this age you'd better move on "something" before you're a "Grandpa Reeves," who used to own this house sixty years ago! He was wild in his last days, marrying a younger woman who I am sure got most of his money. He would sexually chase her around with a rubber-cupped dart gun, trying to hit some erogenous zone he fantasized about, aging happily, and wanting to do more before his death. He was a total "terror" for he was here the longest, and one of the original money-people that bought the property and started the Lake Club. Lee's grandparents were early buyers too. You could only stay for a maximum of six months at your "American" home on the Canadian shores. There were several houses Lizzy and I wanted to buy, but we really didn't need one for having our standing "life-long" invitations.

I could see Lee through the window, fixing my vodka as he stared at Kim popping around in the kitchen with Amanda, Lizzy and Sally. They have the music turned up, and Lee was unnoticeable to them as he made my drink. Duke was getting a platter of stakes ready for the grill.

Duke came out to the porch with Lee, and my drink.

"She's really cute," Lee said.

"Yes, she is, unless she's having a bad hair day, then the bitch comes out!" I laughed.

"She's here alone . . . Where's the guy at your parties in the city?"

"Freddie has to stay in the city. He's about the third flash-in-the-pan for her now since her ex-husband's dead."

"Doe she always act like this?" Lee continued. I knew where he was going with this.

"When she has enough to drink and not on her period. She can be quite neurotic, just to give you advance notice."

"She does like to jump around though!"

"Yep, that she does. We call it the hump-around. Why don't you ask her out sometime?" I said.

"You think she'd go?"

"With your money and her serious need for attention all the time, probably."

"We'll see," is all Lee could say for the moment.


We had dinner then our after-dinner drinks. Nick, Duke and I were in the living room watching the Weather Channel in case we chose to sail tomorrow, and we could see the shadows of Lee talking to Kim outside on the porch through the window screens, explaining the distant lights on the lake. Lee was making some kind of move, as Nick and I were making jokes about the "stumbling" possibilities. Seeing these two together was not on anyone's radar screen and certainly not on Kim's anytime before now. Lee needs to get laid, and Kim was getting enough practice at that lately to open his eyes if that ever happened. Lee was almost a virgin being so sheltered growing up. I think I was in his house only four or five times back then and certainly not within recent years. I would love to play on his clay courts again, for they were the best, and Kimmie could make the fourth if Lee hooked up with her. And this would be a stitch if he balls Kimmie.

Duke didn't quite get some of our comments about the matching but laughed at Nick's and my topics about Lee's un-sexed life. I guessed I could have used some golf jokes to help him make a parallel, but this was happening so quickly tonight that the thought didn't even cross my mind as it happened. Nick and I made several bedroom jokes about looking for a light switch and condoms in the dark.

Duke was now laughing hard enough that he'd wheeze then cough heavily at a few of the really funny ones. I asked him if he was all right a couple of times. He said he was fine, and this was some real funny stuff that Nick and I we're making up. I seriously noted his coughing though.

Our materials for jokes now could only get better, if that ever happened. Nick and I both thought that because if it happened, Lee would have to tell us all the details too. Not telling someone would kill him, for it would be his greatest feat in his single, adult life, and we were there egging him from the onset of his masculine attempt to get the first date. I doubt that Lee can even dance, but I'm sure he'd be content watching!

Lizzy agreed with me that night in bed, recanting our Weather Channel jokes about Lee getting a "good breeze" from Kimmie before we went to sleep that night. She supported our play to make Kim happy again with one of our old friends. We knew Freddie may never be back, for he had no money, just real good sex and dancing to offer.

I'm not sure when married people's matchmaking skills come into play, but we all do it for those singles in our circle of friends. But Lee and Kim? I believe that Lizzy actually thought this would be good, but she really doesn't know Lee at all. She just assumes that Lee is rich and normal, which is basically true with the reality of being a virgin. I wasn't on his "court" then, so I am not really sure if he's ever been laid. He's not smart enough for what he's about to do though, for Kim probably would tie him up with his own socks! I must say that this is the most unlikely thing to happen, for Kim is really an obnoxiously drunken ass with some serious mental insecurities, as surely as the morning dew covers the grass. Lee's quite a bit slower, but he's a really nice guy.

This would be major though, if Lee became "General Lee" to tell his new *first-time* sex stories to us. The details of the accomplishment Nick and I would ask, knowing full well that he couldn't hold back if he wanted to when alone on our boats, tennis courts or cocktails together anywhere and asked to him directly. And now most definitely, tennis would be at his house just so he could tell us these sex tales firsthand. There would be no one there other than his paid help. The girls would know, maybe, heard directly from Kim, like Nicky and I would from Lee. It hasn't happened yet, but those are now our thoughts. Lizzy and I talked about it before we went to sleep that night.

Summer had raced through fall and the weather had turned to winter. We were back in the city again, handling our respective jobs and planning for the next get-together at our house before the long-awaited summer season. Nick and Sally had an open invitation to stay at our city house, party or no party.

Kim had been over a lot during the week and had Freddie on her tail once or twice. She certainly was using her cards for sex with Fred, but I could tell that they were distancing, for he was now more possessive then ever, and I knew that she wasn't enjoying anything other than the sex, according to Lizzy. She was using him as her boy-toy—there was no doubt about that. It was only a matter of time before that would be over.

We were in our kitchen, minus Freddie, chatting over cocktails around 5:30 one evening.

"Hey, let's have the party at my house this time," Kim started saying.

Lizzy and I looked at each other, thought for a second and knew that would be good. Parties are always a big clean up and a bit costly.

"Good, let's do that," Liz said.

"Sure, that'll be good, Kimmie. We'll just keep the same group we were planning."

"I'm not having Fred, okay?"

"I don't care . . . why not?" I asked.

"He's becoming way to common for me. All he wants is to lie around."

"I thought you liked that."

"They're not a good match . . . do you think we should invite Lee?" Lizzy asked me.

"Fine with me."

There it was—some kind of game these girls were setting up. I swear they talk about more shit in the bathroom than us men will ever know. But having the party at Kim's was a great idea, with no coordinating hassles other than to make sure Lee was officially invited.

"Nick and I could always ask Lee to have it at his house. He has shit-loads of money and can afford us," I jokingly suggested, knowing their attempted plan now.

"Stop that!" Kim tartly said.

"I'm kidding. So you like Lee now? And that's why no more Freddie? You're a bad girl . . . and I'm not your dad."

"He seems real nice, Jon. They might like each other," Liz said.

"I know Lee would. And you'd like his money, Kim, don't kid me. You probably saw that 'virgin-like' politeness of his, and it turns you on—*not to mention all that money.* You can't imagine how much."

"So what's wrong with that?" Liz chimed in.

"As I said, I'm not her dad. He's on the list. This should be fun. Boy, that must have been some chat at the lake! It's at your house for seven. Just make sure you have enough rum and vodka for us sailors and Canadian beer for Lee."

And there you have it: the girls had set their plan and goals into dedicated action.

Kim married this man by the end of the year. What a fucking lottery winner she is now. Lee has more money than Amanda, and that's a fact. His beach house blows hers away without comparison, *and Amanda had a real nice beach house.* I wasn't complaining. Nick and Sally had a pleasant one too, but their atmosphere of indulgence was the Lake Club's moorings, tennis courts, dining facilities and boathouse.

The wedding was at Lee's city club, and it was huge. Three hundred plus people came. Everyone came from the lake, even those that I hadn't seen since being a kid, and their children and parents too. It was a real show—one you'd never forget as long as you live. The entire Lake Club was on the guest list and dozens of city folks too.

Lee had spent a wad on this one, and I was astonished because he was always so reluctant to spend a dime without his parent's approval when we were kids eating lunch there or even as being older getting drinks at the club's bar. I don't think I ever saw him buy a drink for someone unless it was payment for a bet, losing to him in some weekly regatta. Some of these guys take sailing way too seriously, much like our women were taking golf now. Our country clubs in the city are a nice place to have lunch and dinner and mostly now, for the wife's golf outings.

Some of these old-timers, our grandparents and such, were rumored to have gotten the big money from their parent's bootlegging days. Nobody knows anything, but the shortest distance across the lake from Canada to Buffalo is here on the Niagara River, at the end of Lake Erie. Money was not the factor at our clubs, in the city or on the lake—"luxury, convenience, and show" were.

Kim was lapping it up like a pleasured cat. Lee just said yes to everything she wanted, including fabulous clothes and vacations, without caring if it was vacation time or not. He'd do whatever she wanted, whenever and with a blank check paying for everything.

After a time, I could see that the money was dramatically changing her.

She was now walking into our parties dressed better than Madonna and flaunting new hairdos. She did do less "poof dances" because she didn't need to—she looked the part on the onset, but when she did, the hair-thing got so outrageous that I all I could think of was the line from Gloria Swanson in the movie *Sunset Boulevard*: "I'm ready for my close up, Mr. De Mill." Kim's eyes were almost the same when she had enough to drink, putting her over the edge; and we all had staircases to come down. Her limits of reality seemed not to exist anymore. If you didn't have enough money, then she was simply right, so she thought. You can never argue with the newly rich in their blind exhibition of expressed money. She simply forgot where she came from and how to treat her friends if it didn't suit her fancy. I felt sorry for her because it made her so much less of a person. Snobbery benefits no one. And newly acquired snobbery was the worst, for it was insulting after it got old. Marriage and money . . . it never works: when one marries for money, it's usually because someone is lying emotionally and not sharing their true feelings. This applies to Amanda for sure!

Like Nick and I first talked about, this was very interesting. I wondered if they needed the light switch to find that first condom that first night "doing it." Lee wasn't the type to have one in his wallet, ever; it'd be in an unopened box in his dresser drawer.

I certainly never expected to see firsthand how money corrupts someone so quickly (before this). Especially after Freddie and the boys' Kim ran-through in succession; Kimmie didn't want to make any compromises. I put her in the "same boat" with Amanda, the spouse stealer. But in Kim's case—she's a "wallet stealer" who went out and took the most money she could find, whether she had a match or not. Amanda simply bought her men, and it was hard to say who was worse—the gold digger or the person with the gold mine selling so unexpectedly and simply cheaply to have *real* love, especially in the eyes of God. I didn't care what state they signed their papers in . . . it seemed wrong.

How Lizzy supported it all was beyond me, other than my having met these two women through her, and I wasn't going to upset that applecart yet. Sticking your nose in previous, unknown friendships wasn't my style of cards. And these three were playing in all of our club's golf scrambles now. I'd voice my opinion, just without any projections for required outcome. Liz and I talked about it, systematically, and that was that—just talk between us with no clear response on her part; it always was at the end of an evening, while in bed.

Where are the morals in life? They do not have exceptions for certain circumstances like someone calling for a mulligan on the golf course. If we all agreed, there'd be one, but if we were in a match play, it is out of the question. Just count your stroke and move on—simply no exceptions. Why keep score if you don't count every stroke? That's not sport; it's cheating. Just count the fucking strokes if we're keeping score. There's no bad-serve-do-overs on the tennis court or exemptions for missing the course marker when sailing. What you get is what you got! That's probably why golf became eighteen holes because someone needed another nine for another chance to win.

The girls were now playing in Pro-Am's and meeting all the great women golfers. The one thing that did surprise me in women's golf though, was this big craze to be a lesbian on the circuit. Some of the local pros were so blatant about it that they'd openly reference how good-looking some of our women were! And of course, most of these women pros looked like men. They were huge in girth, with stomachs as large as their hips! Their bodies were basically a straight shot from the shoulder down to their thighs. And what's with those haircuts being so short and "butchy"?

We boys referred to them as "dikes on spikes." Don't get me wrong, they can play their games anyway they want to, but Amanda lately was always inviting one to fill in as a fourth on club scrambles, using them to gain the edge to win. Ironically, that's why the game invented handicaps. And there seemed to be a number of "low handicappers" playing our courses lately. If they didn't hate men so much and could keep their opinions about sex to themselves instead of toward our wives, nobody would care. Brazen comments about how good one's wife looks, at my country club, is not acceptable club behavior. If they want to join, they can say whatever the hell they want, for they would have paid for the right. That's why our clubs are private. I'm not anti-anything unless you try to steal someone's mate.

From what I've seen and accepted during recent times in outrageous spousal behaviors, I am happy to be labeled the "conquering pioneer," being gregarious, sometimes over-opinionated, but an honest guy with a great wife and happy life. To me, that's what it's all about. Inner peace and shared harmony. Again, I don't chase nor want to be the Joneses. Knowing them is good enough. If life were *instant*, it would stay the same as today and never change, *ever*. One has to achieve that respectfully too, not by buying or marrying it. You simply can't have the complete package with an underlying, hidden agenda. That never works in *real love*. The divorce rate in America is 51 percent for god's sake. Those of us who have experienced divorce never want to see that fork in the road for our hearts again. Most of the time, you do have a choice, working everything out, but then again, some of the time you just never see it coming.

Everyone was getting older, and we were seeing more death of parents and friends now—that's when we saw so many people together again. These weren't parties; they were condolence rituals for honored friendships. After so many years of association, you attended from your heart and not because you had to. You'd show your respect for the surviving families. You shared your memories and good thoughts of the deceased with them, and one hopes they will do the same for you when your time comes.

Birth brings us into the world, death takes us out and funerals always bring the remaining together. It seemed that many of our friends were getting sick now since Pete died, and let's not forget adding Michael to the mix.

Now Duke had something outrageous about his cholesterol and some kind of lung condition, and Lizzy was getting an irregular stream of flus lately.

Sometimes Amanda would come alone to our parties in the city, leaving Duke behind. He always made it to Amanda's beach house though, and he started to look gaunt and pale, but he'd still volley with me on the courts, just not as often, and we never played a set anymore. We would only volley before we had to stop for he was so winded that we both knew it was time to quit. He enjoyed the exercise though, always comparing it to being on the golf course, walking with his bags.

We laughed about walking during golf, for I would always have reasons for using a cart. They are like bumper carts to me, looking for my ball in the woods. We never damaged a golf cart, although I do remember somebody going over a bunker and into a lake once. Duke is an all right enough of a guy, and I hardly ever thought about his wife and kids anymore, for he always had a smile on his face.

We all simply felt that we should keep living and enjoy what we had, not thinking of sickness and sorrow, knowing that time was closing in on us all. These seemed to be the facts of the life we are all sharing now, not running up and down the sand dunes anymore.

MARK FRANCIS SCHWAB

I still kept the Bloodys going though, on any given morning where we were all staying—at the lake or in the city, and everyone was to have one, and several of us had two or three before we'd start our day of leisure. We longed for these weekends when guests could visit without the interruptions of work and the girl's increasingly scheduled golf outings. Everyone's time became so preciously short, with their commitments now written on calendars. I had only "editorial calendars" to live by.

I could care less about the LPGA schedule. Although I thought Annika Sorenstam certainly can play with the big boys and was quite the beauty, having followed her on a course or two with the girls. But I kept that to myself.

# CHAPTER FIFTEEN

# *Stealing Home Plate*

T HE SEASONS HAVE changed again, and it was a harsh winter in the city. The beach memories flowed at every party with Canadian whiskey, Russian vodka, Puerto Rican rum and Canadian beer. Those that never made it to the lake parties would listen to our tales, hoping for an invite sometime next summer.

And since everyone was using calendars to keep schedules, their opportunity for an invite for tennis doubles or a fourth for golf was working into my favor greatly. That meant overnight stays, for we don't let you start with Bloodys and end with scotch before you drive home. However, someone was always missing from our regular crew through prior commitments they had made, and the new guests made good replacements for them.

I love the lake and all it's meant to me over all these years. It's majestic, with both good and bad people you knew well. At this stage, if the bad ones didn't hurt or bother you, everyone got along just fine. That is the way of life at the lake.

At one of the parties at our house in the city, Nick and Sally were laughing so hard about the "race of the dunes" that we had a good crowd laughing together. I was in my bartender's space, filling everyone's drinks and hand-picking those who were next as they stood shaking the ice in their nearly empty glasses.

Amanda was half listening on the outside of the semicircle but still part of the group. Duke wasn't here. He was going into the hospital shortly for some type of medical tests where you couldn't consume anything for twenty-four hours before, and he didn't want to be tempted by a good spread. At least that was Amanda's story why he wasn't able to attend our party. These parties are so tempting when in attendance, having all the food to sample and the help to wait on you that if there was any peer pressure, you couldn't say no, unless you really had to.

So far this is still the Garden of Eden for me—just don't eat the apple! Everyone here, except Lizzy, the Whinstners and me, if given the opportunity, would. I've never met anyone, even myself, who hasn't once regretted something done in life through young arrogance. And we are still truly sorry for those remembered moments of lapsed judgment "crossing the sun" as in the song the Guess Who sang. Yet we are still having our parties, and Nicky was always in my face at the bar.

"You freek'en slipped mother fucker," Nick said discounting me as the winner of one of our off-the-deck games of football where you dove to catch the ball in mid air before hitting the water.

"Like hell. Duke threw it too far."

"Likely excuse, old man."

"I'm still tougher than you, for I have experience on my side . . . and it was overthrown!"

Duke's throw was the winning catch of the game. I couldn't reach it, and the game was "as many caught within reach." He threw out of reach. It was just one of our games, and of "winning remembrances."

"Right, the deck was wet. You won. Right," I said getting him a new rum and tonic.

"You boys . . . and your challenges," Amanda unexpectedly entered in.

"We like it," Nick immediately said.

I laughed, shaking my head, thinking how amazing our competitive games were. This was a rare form for Amanda to follow so closely with an off-the-cuff comment.

Nick and I believed we actually discovered the "dictionary" games we made up way back then on some frozen, stoned weekend party. We'd open the dictionary, say a word with hyphenation, and then use it in a sentence, real or made up: was it the correct meaning or not? You had to choose yes or no. We kept score, with a total of zero wrong as the winner. I loved that game. I'm not sure Duke would be good at it, but Pete was. He always did well at "dictionary."

"Games, Amanda. That's the fun which keeps you young," I said.

Everyone seemed to want a drink after that thought; so I nodded to the best of our help, who always kept her eye on me being their team leader, to take over the bar, and what a smile she had for taking over the bartender's job. I love happy people. They make life good and fun. People should always be happy, and that starts within your own heart, not from having more then someone else. Anything more than providing for your comfort level is simply unnecessary and changes your persona and way of acting like it has done to Kim—nothing like a silver spoon "shoved" in your ass and liking it. But for her, it became an addiction on top of her drinking. Poor Lee for he knew not what he married, yet Nick and I first joked about it on that starlit night at the lake so long ago.

"Where's the champaign," Kim said, bouncing over, shaking her new oversized, rubbery boob-implants in a too-tight zebra-fabric blouse, holding her glass out in front of those waiting for the bottle chilling in the bucket.

"How's Duke? Is he sick?" she said directly to Amanda who was inching away.

"What . . . ? He's fine—doing tests and needing to fast."

"Hope he's not dying," Kim said callously without even knowing how bad that sounded.

Since she wasn't an original friend from the Lake, I grew not to like her much anymore. She was a better person before she entered this group. She boasted about her weekly psychiatric sessions as if she won trophies, and the more sessions she'd have, the richer she felt. That is a scary thought! I couldn't go there, commenting about this. However, listening to Kim and those boring self-centered ideas, she'd repeat them as if these updates were important news flashes every time she'd talk about them. I know she could read my countenance and knew how much I now disrespected her for marrying someone just for the money and how she's flaunted it in everyone's face.

Kim and I drifted apart on every issue, and I liked her less every time she would show up demanding to be the center of attention. We even had a few words occasionally because she would demand that I pay attention too. She would twist everything as being my fault for never listening to her. I thought about being more direct with her but didn't for that would only fuel more asinine behavior, and I was seeing enough of that. I didn't need drawing her anger in front of Lizzy, who would defend her like she does Amanda now. Money not only corrupted these women but also made them stupidly lost in a forest, not able to see the trees.

Poor Lee, for he never expected to create such a person transformed by his money! He probably didn't even know anyway, this being his first marriage to anyone who gave him unabashed sex without interrupting his scheduled routine-overlord for his properties. His sex was when he wanted it, and Kim simply was satisfying a mechanical need with promises for her next purchases. Her losses would be too great to bite this hand. Nick and I joked about her "having to give" Lee a hand job twice a week so he would always be happy. Ah, the simple pleasures in life: monetary fulfillment and ejaculation. If we all could only share what that meant from achieving those graces ourselves, without the hand of others feeding us.

Duke's medical reports came back and Amanda had to tell us that it was serious—something about blocked and clogged arteries. High cholesterol was all we knew, but when I saw him again, he was now gasping for breath on every movement. His face made you want to tell him about diets, but we knew it was from his medicine, like how Jerry Lewis fought taking those drugs that saved his life yet blew him up like a balloon. This was something serious and much more than just his cholesterol. Duke ate all those sticky buns whenever they were on a plate, when I'd be fixing our Bloodys. Thank god for tomato juice as a food staple and possible prostate helper for the lycopene benefits they possessed!

I saw him about three times after that at the beach parties. He came to them in concession. Then he just "unexpectedly" died of a heart attack on some private golf course one day. We all got the same story, but I think he had a severe heart disease that Amanda wouldn't tell us about from the beginning. She never told us about Pete's health either—come to think about it. I didn't like this thought and where it was going, for that would mean that Amanda was *stealing ailing spouses*. Both Pete and Duke died without us knowing the real truth about how sick they were from the beginning. Amanda wouldn't tell anything regarding their illnesses until they were almost dead.

That certainly would explain how easily she could buy them, wouldn't it? But the real question here is "Was she overlapping them, knowing they would need to be replaced?" Now that's a sick way to always keep yourself from being lonely!

I thought about Duke and that it would be a good way to go if he was in the middle of a fairway shot to the green from his drive. He would have hoped that that was his thought too, if he finished the hole. Duke was a fine man, and I will miss his easygoing way. I just hope Amanda has the decency for covering his "old family" again somehow. She didn't do enough for Pete's, and that says it all about her.

I still love life! I'm truly sorry for those of "us who died" whom we all knew so well and even more so for those who were less honorable who are still alive. Death takes a lot out of us all, no matter when we got together and saw everyone now. We always spoke fondly of everyone, remembering our beloved but deceased friends. That feeling meant more to me than most, as what Nicky and I learned from the beginning growing up. We didn't know how to hate someone then, for we just didn't play with them if they cheated.

Today we allow too many mistakes that are continuations... from some of our friends. And Kim was quickly becoming a person I'd rather not take anymore from. As for Amanda, we'd just have to see who's next on her list.

It was now becoming the year from hell, for Lizzy fell deathly ill. This wasn't good, for if true, there was no known cure yet. The disease could have been inhaled or touched to transmit it. We were doing every test available. The best we could figure is touching something that someone infected. She may have itched her nose or put her finger in her mouth, contracting this unknown strain of deadly virus.

We tried to trace it back to the colds she we was getting last golf season, and as the doctor's said, it was totally possible that it could have infected her then. It has spread into her bone marrow like some cancer and was killing all the white blood cells. And that was making her immune system fail.

We had to treat it like a cancer using the same type of medicines and drugs. These drugs sucked too—who invented chemotherapy? It's effects are worse than the illness. I couldn't believe my eyes how it knocked Lizzy down. I would tear up, watching her sleep in a coma-like state as I sat next to her for hours at a time, waiting for her to wake. I would hold her hand to let her know how much I loved her. I would get her anything and everything if I could, but she couldn't do anything but smile back at me, sitting next to her.

Where do these diseases come from anyway? Who can you blame for spreading this? And what in the world is out there? You never think something like this will affect your life, but here it is infecting my dearest Lizzy. And what if she died? The thought was too great to contemplate other than going with the flow and the medication now. I just had to do my best to keep her content and alive. She wasn't thinking clearly when she came out of her week-long chemotherapy knockdowns. These treatments weren't going to stop anytime soon either, and her mind was slipping further away, and further from us as a team. It's hard to describe, but I guess the best way to look at it was that she didn't recollect things well, and she was taking everything in like a child would. She was losing her ability to reason and simply agreed to anything, hoping to ease her pains.

Amanda had offered to help. In the beginning, it was fine, for she would always make sure someone was with Lizzy if I couldn't be there. Her bringing over deli dishes helped a bit, for I was the only one eating the stuff. Lizzy could not stomach much so she lived on the special milk shakes I'd make her. I put everything in them, and she still lost a ton of weight. My heart was saddened to watch this happen in front of me. I held her in my arms as much as I could, holding back my tears, telling her how much I loved her and that we were going to get through this together. She was on the chemo thing for about a year, on and off for three weeks at a time.

Amanda had suggested that she should take her on trips when Lizzy was feeling better between the knockdowns, in case she died. I thought it was a good idea at the time. Somehow I also thought this would include me too as her husband. It didn't. But since Amanda was paying for these very extravagant excursions like she paid for Pete and Duke, I really didn't have a choice, and Lizzy certainly desired these excursions in our hard times.

In fact, I wasn't even asked, and Lizzy couldn't comprehend my feelings to even discuss this with her.

The first two-week trip to the islands was good for her; you could see her smiles again, but she came home to her chemo schedule and would go down almost immediately after she had her treatment. I would sit by her side as she slept on the couch, which I now made-up for her daily. After she'd wake, I'd take her up to bed about 4:30 p.m., which was now "our daily bedtime."

I would bring her the multi-shake and something solid to try every time she sat up without fail. She slowly got more energy as the days went on, sleeping less, and felt well enough to go for a short drive or walk. She loved to go and get a roadside custard or milkshake at a local stand.

Unfortunately, her taste never came back, not on chemo. Everything tasted like metal to her.

I made the house spotless and sterile at all times. When any of our guests came over, they'd have to wash their hands when they arrived, and if you were sick, you couldn't come into the house. I had read about the immune system's vulnerability, and failure would not happen on my watch. I was adamant about that.

Several trips later with Amanda only, I was now confused as to why Lizzy would come home, collapse on the couch and not put anything away, ever. She did not, maybe could not understand the whole toll this was taking on me. I would clean and prepare everything happily. I started to ask why she wasn't unpacking her bags, other than put into laundry piles the things she expected I would do shortly, even when she still felt good enough to do it herself.

She was becoming a different person that I was seeing when she'd return from her trips with Amanda. But I'd have the house ready for her next round of medicine, figuring whatever I could do to make her life more comfortable. I handled her laundry, but she wasn't thinking clearly, just putting anything anywhere for me to clean, organize, put away and expecting me to ready her bags for the next trip with Amanda. We were now getting exotic vacation mailings to the house regularly. I wasn't invited to go on any of them, for Amanda was not paying my passage to LPGA tournaments across the county and only wanted one person on these trips.

I would try and talk to Lizzy about it when she was a day into the chemo, for its full effects didn't knock her the first day. Those conversations were short, for she didn't want to discuss her trips. Then the drug's effects took hold after a few days, and you could only pray for her, holding her hand as she'd lay almost motionless.

We got heated about a few topics, I must admit. The constant sterilization of the house, the multi-week vacations with only Amanda, our lack of loving companionship and the piles of everything to put away were wearing heavily on me, let alone how ill she was.

"What's the gig, darling? I'll pay my own way. Why don't we all go? I could use a break with you too."

"That's not what this is about. Amanda wants to spend time with me alone. I'm here all the time."

"Really?"

"Yes, I'm home now."

"Isn't tomorrow your injection?

"Yes," she said.

"I'm a bit concerned about not being able to go. Those are nice places, and I'd enjoy sharing the good times too."

"It's not that. Amanda picks up everything, and it would be awkward."

"Awkward? I'd pay for myself," I said.

"Let's change the subject, okay."

"Are you going to be able to do your laundry and put your things away?"

"You know, I will not be able tomorrow . . ."

"Yes, I know that."

All of this didn't make me happy. I was not to go, and it was Amanda's orders. The appearance of this certainly was requiring thought from me—serious thought. Why wasn't Lizzy sharing her "good days" with me too? I knew they both knew each other before I came into the scene, but my partner-in-life is sick with an incurable disease, and simply, she is my wife. I wasn't going to upset the applecart when she was down, without an immune system and on chemotherapy, to make any changes whatsoever. I was still thankful that she's still alive. No matter what though, that fucking Amanda gave her orders that I wasn't allowed to go.

Lizzy's on my watch for better or worse, sickness and health, for richer or poorer, and I won't let those responsibilities slip ever. It's my life with her too, my duty as her husband, even though it's hard to communicate with her for all the drugs she's on. Safety, health and caring are all that I can think about. Amanda is another matter, and I'll not suck-it-up to please that bitch.

"We need to talk about stuff," I said one day when she teturned home from another trip.

"What now? Didn't I get the colors in the right pile? Is it always my fault? I'm sick, damn it. I could die tomorrow."

"Don't talk that way. I'll figure something out for us."

"It's too late, I'm going to die . . ."

"Not yet, you're not."

"Soon."

"Is there something I should stop doing or know about?"

"No," she said.

"Ok then, help me clean a little when you're home . . . don't have chemo the day you come home. Plan for a few days later, and let's share our home together."

"I like these trips . . . they're paid for," is all she said.

That was hard to understand for we were so tight before the chemo thing. I thought we could discuss anything, and eventually agree for some neutral grounds, like good married folks do. Now, we seemed to disagree on everything about anything, including our own schedule of time together. It now had to be written on a calendar—for her chemo-dates and the Amanda trips. Our marriage needed a schedule just to spend healthy times together.

I don't like a marriage where two cannot agree and answer all questions together, for marriage is sacred. Marriage is the constitution to live as one and why you married in the first place. There are no unanswered questions, for everything has its place and purpose, together.

But what in hell Amanda is doing here is very suspicious. She is having too much control of my wife's time that I was going to confront her as intelligently as I could, as a stressed husband under these conditions. And who in the hell would want to ask these questions anyway? It isn't like me to even think something is wrong; yet something was happening between those two and between Lizzy and me.

Who, what, when and where are what we demand in journalism for the topics we write to tell. Without these, it doesn't sell. This didn't sell to me, not after seeing Amanda's stealing of life and death experiences with Pete and Duke. I was heavily concerned about all of this.

*Summer was now in the city, and death was at the Lake*, I started to think. I knew better, if not just for my old friendship with the Whinstners.

Death happens, and so does some bad shit sometimes. Lately, death was more relevant than any of our fun times. It was consuming many of our lives firsthand, so I didn't feel completely alone. We were having significant problems, but Lizzy was still alive, and I am damned determined to keep her that way, no matter what Amanda's plans are.

I am the one you want in the "trench" in warfare, for I will be the one that gets us out alive. I'm a true fighter for that shit. Nobody gives up while I'm alive, fighting next to them. And if you're to come out alive, just watch me and do what a leader says while keeping your head

MARK FRANCIS SCHWAB

down. Not being allowed to vacation too when Lizzy was able, based on Amanda's demand, was really pissing me off.

I began to drink a lot more during her vacations with Amanda. I couldn't get it out of my mind why Liz would go for this: Amanda and her sharing "the good life" without me and then coming home for hospice care during the knockdown chemo sessions. Something was amiss, and I was going to find out what.

Lizzy and I would argue more now than ever about these things. We never had these problems before her incurable disease and the affects of chemotherapy or Amanda's constant presence. That drug fucks up your mind, and Amanda was fucking up our lives, not being my *assistant* care-giver as she first proposed.

Lizzy was now saying things to me that would cut through the soul.

"Why can't you make more money? And stop harping about the house and having to clean everything all the time."

"What do you want me to talk about while I'm cleaning the mess around here? You're off with Amanda all the fucking time, and then you're home lying down in a coma for two weeks . . . and what's with this more money stuff?"

"I'm sick for christ's sake."

"Where am I living, in a bubble? You need to make more time for us, and being sick doesn't give you the right to use me as a slave for getting things ready for another trip with that woman."

"Stop it. I don't need this."

"Need what, where are you going with this?"

"I'll travel whenever I want."

"Yea, and Amanda takes care of everything, except for your husband. She all of a sudden doesn't care about our life here? What else is going on?"

"I'm not discussing this anymore."

"Typical. I'm going to say something to her."

"You'd better not, or else—"

"Or else what . . . you'll take another trip?"

"I'm not taking this—"

"But you'll take Amanda's trip won't you? And I'm not sure exactly what you think we're talking about."

"Stop it," she screamed at me going into the bedroom.

And she did have another trip planned after she recovered from this round of chemotherapy. This trip was to some exotic golf resort in the California Mountains, another LPGA Pro-Am or something like that.

We were seriously drifting apart from any normal conversations. In fact, we hardly had normal conversations anymore, except when she would sit up on the couch, asking for water or one of my milkshakes I kept her alive with.

Where does Amanda get off? I was starting to think about her past relationships, but that thought was unfathomable to be real when applied to Lizzy. The problems and conversations between Lizzy and me were getting more directive and with purposely unanswered questions. It was hard imagining this, but it was happening. Amanda was stealing my wife like she stole Pete and Duke.

Lizzy and I had another dozen arguments on the same topics, and one day she said she was moving out!

"That's it. I'm leaving!"

"What?" is all I could say.

"I'm leaving tonight."

"And where would you be going?"

"None of your business. I can't take all these questions. You need to get happy."

"It's hard being happy when knowing my wife's going to Die, and Amanda is doing her M-O."

"I'm not dead yet, so don't count on it," she said.

I could tell this was something more than just another argument.

"Honey . . ."

"Don't give me that."

"What should I give you?"

"I'm not taking any more questions and your bullshit."

"You never do . . . and what are you and Amanda doing on these trips." I shouldn't have said it but this was getting too cozy for my comfort.

"That's it. I'm leaving."

"Where?"

"Fuck you," was all she said, grabbing a few clothes and sundries.

I tried to reason with her, but the anger between us was just too hard now that our comments were vicious quips just for response. Nobody likes being in the corner, and we both felt that way, for we were not communicating at all. It was more tit for tat than anything real, yet this was really happening. What drugs do they give sick people?

Lizzy got in her car and left that night around 7:00 p.m. I couldn't feel anything after that moment, other than the tears running down my face, trying to call her at someone's house. There were no answers, only voice mail to speak to, which I left as short as possible, trying not to sound like I was crying more than I was. Why we get so mean and angry with such a loved one, I cannot answer. Amanda had planted all this in her. The money, the trips and the anger were coming from Amanda. She is the devil, corrupting life for her own personal needs and companionship without regard for others.

I could not find Lizzy anywhere that evening, and I felt sick to my soul about this. This couldn't be over, it just couldn't. We were so in love for so many years that this wasn't possible. I kept trying to think how to stop all of this, but she had left.

When I finally talked to her two days later, she called to get more of her things. She had moved in with Amanda, and my heart sank when I heard that. This cannot be fucking real, yet it was. She moved in with the *spouse stealer*. My wife! What the fuck was happening here?

"Can I come over and get some things?"

"Liz, of course, but you don't need to get anything—everything's here for you."

"We'll talk. I just want to get some things, okay?"

"I'm sorry, just come home."

"We'll talk. I need a change of clothes."

"Yes, you can always come home. Can you come tonight?"

"Tomorrow at lunch," was all she said hanging up the phone.

That all happened; and then later that month, she came and packed all of her favorite clothes with Kim and a friend, helping her move things out. I felt devastated but was determined to say all nice things. I wanted our life back again, and it seemed pointless for me to say anything petty just to make a point from our past arguments. Amanda was purposely absent from this crew and wasn't part of any discussions.

"Can we come in?"

"You can always come . . . home, honey," was all I could say to Liz, looking into Kim's glaring eyes.

What their friend's name was, I couldn't remember. I had met her on our golf course once but I didn't know her. Lizzy was the first of the three to walk through the door.

"Let's get this done," Kim said, passing me while I held the door open.

"Liz, are you sure about this?" I had to say.

"Listen, divorce happens every day, so get used to it," Kim snapped at me in response.

"Get out of my life, please!"

"You're a loser, and who do you think you are growing your hair that way?" Kim returned.

"Fuck you, Kim. You've become a fat and stupid person. Liz, what on earth are you doing?"

"I'm getting my things," she said climbing the stairs to our room, with the girls right behind her.

This shocked me, for when and where did this path take its turn for this outcome? I was dumbfounded and lost to give more in reply to her actions, with her team fueling their climb. And what stuff was so important to her after so many years of marriage? We owned everything together.

I hated Kim more than ever now and thought even less of Amanda, for my wife had moved in with her. Where are all of our past morals in this marriage? I didn't have to guess for now I knew. It had to be all those "dikes on spikes" trips. And anything here wasn't for me at this moment in time. The deal was done. I had lost her, and it began with her deadly disease. Amanda not only stole spouses, but they all were sick and dying, put under the power of her money. As for Kim, she was spending money to be as fat as Amanda, both in conquest and weight.

I didn't know who I wanted to kill first, Kim or Amanda.

Amanda must have been working on this ever since Liz got sick, just before Duke died. Who would think she would steal a woman this time? She is one sick bitch to plan her life this way, stealing spouses for her own companionship needs. This is sick behavior—classic textbook psychosis.

I had lost my wife for some unwillingness to compromise on daily life that real people compromise on. At least, real married people do without quitting something so sacred as our "I do, for better and worse, until death do you part." Liz had lost all of her reasoning power and was letting the girls do her thinking. And Amanda's money is the root of this evil—that and whatever Lizzy's medications were doing to her.

Nobody could have expected what Amanda planned here, but you can now see why she had always someone in her life. She is manipulative and conniving and has no regrets about who she hurts along the way as long as she gets what she wants. What a fat worthless pig with a lot of money.

Lizzy and I both got attorneys and let them do their thing. When I signed the papers, I could not believe that I was divorced, looking at my now ex-wife across the lawyer's table.

What the fuck does it matter now, other than losing something and moving on again? Not my choice and something I hope to forget sometime; its pain runs through my body. Three marriages now. Am I wrong to have wanted to save them all?

All I felt now was for selling any shared property to save my soul, and using it to pay our attorney's rounds of golf at their country club for the next several years with what they have charged each of us!

I could only think of Kenny Loggins' lyrics: "I bet you wish you could cut me down with those angry eyes . . . what a shot you'd be, with those angry eyes," as I looked at Liz one more time walking out of the attorneys office, papers in hand.

The loss of our shared family and several of the friends happened quickly because everyone had to take sides on this one. It was a war that ended, and everyone was a loser.

# CHAPTER SIXTEEN

## *Pressed from Past to Future*

A T THIS MOMENT, I can only quote that line from *Gone With the Wind* when Scarlet grabbed a handful of dirt at the end of the movie: "After all, tomorrow is another day!"

That day is today and that I have to keep reminding myself to move forward. I have to accept reality face-on again, for tomorrow *will* be another day too. I'm divorced and single, just older and wiser from the last; how much more wiser from the second than the third, I'm not sure. But if I ever marry again, it would make too many times from the beginning.

Marriage is not on the list. I'm not in any rebounding mood after this last one, if I can help it, and a loved lost the third time around can be written up to rebounding. Accepting that love of family and friends again cannot be easily had, needing a much greater contemplation for who you would say "I do" to again—words spoken to complete the ritual or a document you both sign to be legal and are said too easily to suit current situations. I'm going to have them check their baggage at the door and simply shoot any Amanda types, if not just to put them out of misery.

There were no divides with the Whinstners this time, and I was certain that they would always be my friends hereafter. We've seen the birth of the Lake's children together, and I could only hope any new parents do not do what "all the parents" did to us as children here at the lake. They virtually handed us the keys to the liquor cabinet and all the toys! Except for Lee's of course.

In remembering those very young days, parents should have known not to leave their kids alone, all together at one of the houses. We've always been allowed to have parties and use the "supplies" just so they knew we'd stay home while they partied at the Lake Club. And when they'd call, we'd tune down our underage parties, otherwise it was sex, booze and all! If love and living life were that easy for everyone, we'd all live it. And even here at the lake, it gets screwed up.

I know I will try to love again, for I love what love is: sharing emotional togetherness, respected wonderments and meaningful sex together. I'm just not sure how to go about having that right now though. It's hard to imagine such a commitment. My soul and visions have changed so much since the first time. And now, this Lizzy and Amanda thing was just unfathomable.

Love is more of a lifelong quest for revelation and truth. Living life today cannot answer that so seamlessly now after three marriages. There are no answers. Looking from within, regaining self-respect when you look into the mirror is what I am looking for. You can't take the achievements away though, and I'm just as proud of the past as I am with moving into the future while controlling my emotions as an adventurous endeavor—if we only knew that way back then, life would be instant.

The Whinstners have an open invite for me this summer, and we were planning to have fun like we did on all the boats and at the dunes. Sally's love for Nicky is a great gift to him, and we all smiled again as we did as childhood friends. They had married the right person from the beginning.

One night, we started talking about me dating again. I could see where this was going, and God bless happy people playing matchmaker, for that's what they were driving at. And I didn't have a problem with this.

"We have this really great friend, don't we, Nick?" Sally said to me sitting on their porch.

The lake had a glistening reflection from the moon over it. It's funny when things look so perfect on such quiet warm nights. I wasn't planning anything, and that's why it happens.

"Is she cute?"

"She's dead gorgeous," Nick made the point.

"Dead gorgeous?"

"Dead gorgeous. A little crazy like you though . . . and single," Sally said.

"I am willing to try a date."

"Damn right you are . . . get off your rocker old man. You'll love her, she's a knockout buddy-boy," Nick said before Sally could say anything.

"She's recently divorced," Sally said.

"We're in the same boat then. Let's do dinner at the club!"

We all were smiling and felt happy about me meeting Tracy, their friend. She is also a resident visitor like me and was staying on the weekends at another of our friend's house for now, just off the beach. From what I guessed, she has been a "resident-visitor" up here for about two or three years now, just not in our last circle. I felt comfortable in the Whinstners' company and staying at their home, and they liked having me as their guest. I was not boring and they wanted me to meet her.

Tracy and I hit it off like no tomorrow. We started doing a ton of things and went to all the old haunts all around the lakeshore. She loved to walk to the dunes on the west shore on the "secret" paths other than sailing there with Nick and Sally. These paths were now crossing private properties that were becoming more private every day.

Nick and Sally sometimes would join us for picnics on the dunes, for they hadn't walked the path in years either, and they enjoyed the woods too. It was exercise for all of us, with growing memories to share on future nights at the club's bar.

Tracy and I loved our times alone at the dunes though. It was a timeless sanctuary from our passed married memories. We'd sit arm in arm at the shores' edge, watching small waves drift over our feet. The water felt almost baptismal as we smiled with love into each other's eyes. We had become closer than I thought we could, and I wasn't sure about anything other than wanting to thank Nick and Sally for hooking us together.

One day, I just said to Tracy something astonishingly real, in this early stage of our growing friendship.

"No more sex for a while. We don't need to have it. It'll just ruin everything. I want to love you that much, and sex will just mess everything up. Let's try being platonic together for a while."

"Say that again."

"You heard what I said, let's be best friends and not ruin anything right now. It will be our measurement to test the value of what we think we're sharing."

She thought about it for at least ten minutes as we enjoyed this moment of my truthfully spoken words to her. Sex always screws things up, and I liked Tracy too much to have that happen. I felt that we could just eliminate that challenge, at least for now.

She agreed, even after I wanted to change my mind, and that became our reality for a while. We still joke about it today. The Whinstners fully understood how much we loved each other, and we were always on their guest list together. I only wished that I could have understood all of this then, when I thought I knew love from the very first time. Tracy and I were permanent partners and welcome nomads at the lake.

I will remain single for a long while, enjoying life and sharing good times with my true friends. Those desk drawer numbers will always remain uncalled, for my feelings were for Tracy and her alone.

Death takes us out, rebirth brings us into something good, and the funerals always get the last of the living together. There were fewer to see at those gatherings now, and anyone of us could be next.

At my age, those games with Nick on the dunes or diving off his boat to catch a football were fun but now too physically demanding, and we'd talk about them at every outing. The "healing" time is just too much for injuries and is stronger than any selfish desires we've lost or gained in those momentary triumphs.

Lizzy had died earlier in the year, and I felt a tremendous loss in my heart. But as for Amanda, I couldn't give a damn whom she would steal again, for what comes around goes around. Her methods have been exposed for what she is—a stealer of married people who are ill and cannot fight for themselves. She lures them in through systematic, financial cajolement and takes full advantage during their catastrophic weakness that they couldn't help it, making her money seem more powerful than it is. Her punishment is that she will always be alone, as long as she lives.

Lenord woke up one day to Kim's bullshit and divorced her. That added a little happiness to my heart for now she'd have to be a real person again, and Lee would continue being a friend as we were from our early days growing up together here, on the Canadian-American shores.

One evening at the Whinstners, after a long summer day's sail, we were finishing our last cocktails for the evening on the porch, looking out over the lake. Tracy was going home and coming over in the morning for Sunday brunch.

"Let's take our coffee on the shore tomorrow," I said holding hands, walking her to her car.

"Love you baby," she said.

I kissed her good night and walked back to Nick and Sally's house, thinking only of the words in one of Crosby, Stills, and Nash's songs: *"You must have a code to live by . . . so teach your children well."*

## THE END

CPSIA information can be obtained
at www.ICGtesting.com
Printed in the USA
BVHW030500160820
586536BV00016B/19

9 781453 577127